Bottom Line Publications

Presents

Good Girls

Bounce Back

<u>**A NOVEL BY**</u>

Eric Lamont Williams

ISBN- 979-8601806473

Edited By: Eric Lamont Williams

Cover By: Iesha Bree "coversmyway.com"

Facebook: Bottom Line Publications LLC (Please Follow)

ACKNOWLEDGMENTS

I want to dedicate this book to everybody who looked at me like I was crazy when I told them the ideas I had for this book. Many people didn't have hope in me, but by the grace of God I was able to put this book together. Thanks to my big sister Tajuanda who never lost hope in me. I live everyday trying to be the best I can be and through my writing is where I find my peace and escape from the world. Thank you to everyone who opens this book far enough to read this page and I'm hoping you'll turn more pages. I really appreciate your support! Be blessed and never let anyone tell you that you can't do anything. Shout out to my pops too, Tyreese Taylor thanks for always giving me the drive to accomplish and though you're far away you're still in my heart always. Always follow your dreams!

INTRODUCTION

Sasha woke up for work doing her normal six o'clock in the morning routine. She turned her favorite song on her mp3 player and got ready for a shower. After her shower, she got on her knees and prayed with just her towel wrapped around her before getting dressed. Sasha ironed her hair out, put on her lip gloss and headed out the door after getting dressed. She worked for Nordstrom in Circle Centre mall, downtown Indianapolis, Indiana. Even in her work uniform you could still see the outline of her amazing body figure. She wasn't your average nineteen-year-old. Sasha really had a solid and beautiful future ahead of her. She graduated from Warren Central High School with honors and had recently taken her SAT's to be accepted into UCLA. Her dream was to get a master's degree in Business Management and someday own her own business. Though she had many offers from colleges all over the United States her goal was to get to the Sunshine state of California, where she could also try her hand in acting. Sasha's upbringing was good with not much trouble at all. Both of her parents worked hard to get along because they made a promise they would stay in the same household until Sasha was eighteen, but her father had passed away her senior year of high school. After his passing Sasha and her mother occupied the house her father left for her in his estate, which was the same house she grew up living in all her life. Sasha never looked at the house as hers and her mother never looked at it like it was Sasha's neither, her mother stayed in control of everything as usual, she didn't care what was left for Sasha.

Sasha arrived at work being her everyday self with a smile on her face that would light up any dark day and had a great attitude to match. She was a cashier but doing other jobs around the store was nothing new to Sasha because she was always all over the place making sure things were in place. Most of her coworkers loved her and she loved them the same, the only coworkers who didn't like Sasha was the few women that resented her. Growing up she had a best friend named Rebecca and they were still best friends. Sasha greeted her customers with respect, and they greeted her with respect. Things were really going good for Sasha at work. Many men tried to take her out, but Sasha would decline every one of them being that she was focused on her career. She would date here and there but would never commit to no man. She made a promise to her parents that she would wait until marriage for sex and do things according to the word of God. With so many things on her mind a man just didn't stay on her mind for long.

Sasha's high school sweetheart Ronald stayed in her memories, but after she caught him cheating on her she lost interest in him. He pressured her for sex, but she never fell for it, so he got sex from other women and ended up getting caught. Though Ronald did stay on her mind she promised to never let him hurt her again, so she kept her distance. She knew she could have had practically any man she wanted so men were the least of her worries. She and her best friend Rebecca had their lives already planned out in which Rebecca was enrolling in UCLA as well.

Sasha was putting some items on the shelf when a male customer approached her and asked her if she could ring his items up and check him out. Though there were many other female clerks around he had his eyes fixated on Sasha. With no hesitation, Sasha told him, "yes sir" and headed for her cash register. The man stood around six foot four inches tall and was a giant compared to Sasha, which she stood only five foot six inches. Many of her female coworkers were looking at this man lusting, but he was just a customer in Sasha's eyes. This man was a man that any woman would fall for. He was tall, dark, muscular, and had all the other nice features women craved. You could tell he was about his business plus had class by the Armani suit he wore and his well-groomed vocabulary. His cologne smelled good and he put it on just right you could smell it strong, but at the same time you couldn't smell it strong. As Sasha walked in front of him, he smiled as he looked down to see her rear end bounce left to right. Sasha's athletic figure with her well-rounded buttocks made most men stop dead in their tracks just as he did while still trying to keep up with her.

Sasha got to her register and started typing her passcode in to operate the register. Other women were more than happy to serve him, and they made it known, but he just smiled and let them know that he was waiting on Sasha to type her code in to serve him. That made the women look at him and roll their eyes, because they knew Sasha wouldn't give no man the time of day anyway. They knew that about Sasha, but obviously, he didn't know by the way he looked at her and smiled, like he really had a chance.

CHAPTER 1

As Sasha grabbed his first two shirts to ring up, she smiled at the man and introduced herself as Ms. Williams.

"Well, hi Ms. Williams, my name is Nick. By the way you have the most beautiful smile I've seen since my mother passed away."

Sasha smiled and said, "Thanks for the compliment sir and I'm very sorry to hear about your mother. I lost my father a little while back, so I know how it feels to lose a parent."

They had small talk until she was done ringing up his items and began to bag the items up.

Then Nick asked, "Will you be willing to go on a date with me?" Before she could answer his question, he said, "Well, sorry I didn't even ask if you were involved with anyone, I don't see a ring, so I doubt that you're married?"

"No, I'm not involved with anyone, but I'm not interested in a date, though I do appreciate the offer sir," Sasha said as she thought to herself that she didn't want to be disrespectful.

"Well, here's one of my cards with my personal number on it and my business number as well, if you happen to change your mind you can give me a call, I'll never forget you. And it'll be in your best interest to call, Ms. Williams," said Nick with a determined look on his face.

Sasha took the card and told him thank you even though she had no intentions of ever calling him.

Nick then said, "Would you mind me having your first name Ms. Williams?"

"My first name is Sasha," she said as she handed him his bags and his receipt and went on to say, "thank you for shopping at Nordstrom and please shop again, sir, we appreciate your business."

Though his total was over a thousand dollars and he paid in cash it didn't impress Sasha because she wasn't into money like most of her female coworkers.

"Pretty name for a pretty woman, you have a great day as well Sasha, I look forward to taking you out one day. I hope you use the number," said Nick as he walked away from the register with a smile on his face.

The other women Sasha worked with ran over to her once Nick walked out asking her what he said. She told them he had given her a card that she was about to dispose of, and they looked at her like she was crazy.

Her coworker Tonya went on to say, "girl you need to quit turning away these fine ass men, you can give them all to me." Tonya said this with a smile on her face as she started to twerk a little.

Sasha just smiled and walked away from them to finish stocking the shelves. She thought to herself that these women had no morals about themselves. She remembered her mother always told her that men could be deceiving no matter how flattering their appearance was. Sasha's mother told her when she met her father, they were both using public transportation and just so happened to meet on the bus. Sasha knew that everything her parents had they worked very hard together as a team to achieve and she wanted the same type of marriage when she was to meet the man of her dreams.

While Sasha was stocking shelves, she could hear a few of her coworkers talking about her. She was used to it, but it did hurt her feelings that they smiled in her face but talked behind her back. In her heart, she felt she was more than a friend to them, and she constantly went out of her way for them. She would let them borrow money and give them rides to and from work when they needed her, without ever accepting their gas money. She also never complained when they needed her to cover their shifts for them. In her years of growing up her parents had taught her about these types of women, so she still treated them with respect as she wanted respect herself.

Sasha could hear Tonya telling her other two coworkers Christina and Michelle, "That bitch must think her shit don't stink with her spoiled ass."

Then Michelle said, "She really isn't all that to me anyway, I don't know why all these men look past us and look at her."

That's when Christina said, "She must like women with her stuck-up ass. They only want her ass because she got that high school pussy anyway." After that they all laughed and went their separate ways.

Sasha's only friend was Rebecca, and Rebecca embedded in Sasha's mind for years that women will always hate what they can't be, so Sasha just learned to let statements like that bypass her. Many people thought Sasha and Rebecca had sexual relations, but they were just best friends and nothing more. Rebecca was very beautiful herself, but Sasha seemed to get all the attention from men for some reason. Rebecca never had a problem with that because she looked at Sasha as a sister. Though Rebecca had been hurt herself she still fully gave another man a shot and he pleased her. Sasha was just waiting for the right man to come along, so she could be happy with a mate like her best friend was. Sasha stayed focused on her career, knowing that when a man was meant to be in her life, God would send him without her putting in any effort.

As the day went on, Sasha was called to the manager's office, which the manager was a man who admired her in a sexual way, but he also honored the business side of Sasha. First, she didn't know what to think, she was nervous because she did take Nick's business card, but she braced herself and walked towards his office. While on the way to his office all her coworkers who so called liked her but were jealous of her waved to her. In their minds, they all hoped she was on her way to get fired. Sasha gave them a smile and went on her way. She tried not to look nervous, but inside she was really scared because this was her first time being called over the intercom to the manager's office.

Sasha knocked and was told to come into the office by her manager, Mr. Jackson. As she walked in, she said, "Good afternoon Mr. Jackson."

"Good afternoon gorgeous, have a seat," he said motioning for her to sit down. Mr. Jackson always flirted with Sasha, but she never told on him.

As Sasha sat down, she said, "Please don't tell me I'm in trouble, I really need my job."

"Oh, no Sasha, as long as I'm here you'll always be here, you're my favorite worker and one day hopefully you'll be my wife," said Mr. Jackson as he flirted trying to get an expression out of Sasha, but all he got was the blank stare he always got.

Sasha just let the flirtatious statement go and said, "well, it's great to know that I'm not in trouble."

"Actually, I called you in to let you know that I'll be leaving the company within forty-eight hours for a better paying job at Rue 21, but I was asked who I thought could fill my shoes and I gave corporate your name," said Mr. Jackson.

"Please don't play with me sir this is great news if you're serious," Sasha said as she cracked a puzzled smile.

"To show you how serious I am, I'll go ahead and make the call to tell them that you accept, and you'll be the immediate intern store manager," he said as he picked up the phone to make the call.

As Mr. Jackson grabbed the phone Sasha sat there with a million and one things going through her mind. She thought about the fact that she would be going off to college in a matter of months. She also thought about the fact that she would be locking in a career and not just a job with the store manager's position. A normal day at work for her now would be a full day of decision making. As store manager, she knew she would make a nice salary, but with the career she dreamed of after she was to finish college, she knew she would make an even better salary. Either way, she knew she was in a tough situation and had to thoroughly think things out.

"Yes, she said she is willing to step up as intern," said Mr. Jackson as he talked on the phone.

Mr. Jackson hung up the phone after writing down a few notes from the phone conversation. He had a big liking for Sasha. He knew he was wrong for trying to get with her, being that he and her father were good friends back in the day. Mr. Jackson even knew her mother, but if Sasha had given him a chance, he just figured he would have a lot of explaining to do. Above all, he knew he would marry Sasha in the drop of a dime, no matter who he had to explain something to.

Mr. Jackson handed Sasha the paper he had been writing notes on, and said, "Well, here is the phone number to reach corporate and Mr. Shepard wants you to call him first thing tomorrow morning."

Sasha replied with, "I want to thank you so much for choosing me of all the people you could have chosen." You could see the excitement in Sasha's eyes as she tried to keep her smile concealed. Mr. Jackson loved Sasha's beauty, so he just stared at her as she smiled.

"I know I may flirt with you and say some thing's I shouldn't say to you, but Sasha your performance is what made me choose you. Your attendance is impeccable, and you've never had the least bit of a complaint filed against you by a customer. I want to see you succeed because hard workers can sometimes be overlooked, but I'll see to it that you don't go through the stage of being unnoticed," said Mr. Jackson as he stood up to shake Sasha's hand.

Sasha stood up and put her hand out to shake Mr. Jackson's hand and said, "Thank you and I will never forget this."

Sasha smiled and turned around to leave Mr. Jackson's office. The door shut behind her and she proceeded to go to the front of the store. As she approached the front of the store her coworkers looked to see what type of facial expression she had on her face. Sasha always had the same look on her face so they couldn't tell what was on her mind. Then one of her female coworkers who really did like her walked up to her.

"Sasha, I heard you were about to get fired and I'm trying to make sure that's a lie," said Drea as she popped her gum with her hands on her hips. Drea was one of those women who spoke her mind no matter what. Many people looked at her like she was ghetto, but Drea was just Drea. Drea was surely a woman you would want to have on your team, her bloodline should have been named loyalty. She was loyal to everyone she loved and always went that extra mile for them. On the flip side, though, she didn't take any stuff from anybody.

"No, I didn't lose my job Drea, thank you so much for your concern," replied Sasha.

"See these hoes in here just don't know how to mind their business. Had me worried talking about you got called to the office because you took some fine ass man number. These hoes are just messy with their ugly asses," said Drea as she turned around to walk away. Drea had a booty out of this world and even a woman couldn't help but to comment on it. Sasha was strapped, but Drea was in a league of her own when it came to the buttocks area.

Drea stopped walking after Sasha called her name to stop her from walking away. She went back and Sasha started to explain to her what happened in Mr. Jackson's office.

"Mr. Jackson called me in his office to tell me that I was chosen to take over the store because he is taking a position with another company," said Sasha.

"Girl, I am so proud of you," said Drea as she hugged Sasha. All the other women were just looking and trying to figure out what was going on. They all knew not to make Drea mad, so they didn't do anything out of the ordinary.

"Drea it surprised me so much because I've never been called to the office over the intercom," Sasha said as she hugged Drea back.

"These hoochies out here had your name all in their mouth girl, I didn't know what to think." Then Drea turned around and said in a loud voice, "to all you hoochies, no she is not fired, Sasha will be you hoes new boss," Drea said as she smiled at Sasha and started to do a celebratory dance shaking her booty and throwing her hands in the air.

Sasha was the humble type of woman, so she really tried not to say anything or seem overbearing. Drea on the other hand was raised on the eastside of Indianapolis in a neighborhood called Trife Life where you had to have a dominate attitude or you would get ran over. Sasha was from a nice neighborhood; it wasn't where the rich folks stayed at, but it was nice and peaceful. It was off 21st and Franklin Road also on the east side of Indianapolis. They both went to the same high school, however they never really said much to each other. Not because they didn't like each other, merely because they lived totally different from one another. Once Drea came to Nordstrom and started working with Sasha they became cool and started to have conversations with each other.

"Please calm down for me Drea," said Sasha as she gave a shy grin.

"No girl you need to let these hoes know because you don't bother anyone so these hoes shouldn't be bothering you."

"Okay, well I'm a get back to work Drea, I love you girl," said Sasha as she turned around and headed for the aisles of the store quickly.

"I love you too girl," Drea said as she turned and went her own way switching her butt cheeks from right to left on purpose.

The other women were just staring at Drea wondering what she meant when she said that Sasha would be the new boss. Drea was very attractive, but she didn't get as much hate as Sasha because she was known for being a good fighter and would check anyone in a heartbeat. Though Drea and Sasha didn't hang much outside of work they were still very close.

During work, they talked about any and everything, so they had a bond in their own way. They also had many mutual friends, being that they went to the same high school. One thing for sure is that Drea wouldn't let anything happen to Sasha under her watch.

Before you knew it Drea was running around telling everyone the news about Sasha being the new boss. Sasha didn't like to boast and brag, but she set herself up for it considering she told Drea first and Drea was known for rubbing stuff in people faces. After a while people started to catch Sasha by herself and ask if the rumor was true. When she said yes, you could see the hate in their eyes. This meant to most of them that they would be finding another job because they didn't like Sasha, and surely didn't want her to be their boss.

"Hey Sasha, I heard you're going to be the new boss, what's going to happen with Mr. Jackson," asked Tonya as she approached Sasha with a puzzled look on her face?

"Yes, I will be acting store manager for who knows how long, but I'm pretty sure Mr. Jackson will tell everyone the details of why this has come about. It's really not my place to tell anyone else's business," replied Sasha.

"Well, I know you're going to start firing people so let me tell you that I'm sorry for any misunderstanding we may have had in the past," said Tonya.

"I'm not firing anyone Tonya; my job is to make sure this store is operated correctly and to make sure every customer has a smile on their face when they walk out of here. I have no personal problems with anyone here so please don't think that way Tonya," said Sasha as she reached out to shake Tonya's hand.

"Thank you, Sasha," said Tonya as she shook Sasha's hand. "You know I'm going to be real with you Sasha you're not a bad person and I should have never taken anyone else's opinion and judged you before I knew you for myself."

When Tonya started working for Nordstrom, she fell right in with all the women who were hating on Sasha. Although she never knew Sasha for herself, she still believed the other women and started disliking Sasha just like the other women. Now she was feeling different about Sasha after seeing that she was really a soft-spoken person.

Sasha replied with a simple, "thank you and you never know sometimes, girl."

As they went their separate ways Sasha went into deep thought. Her first thought was that she needed to call her best friend Rebecca to tell her the news. Sasha knew from experience with her best friend that she would analyze the whole situation and ask her what she would do about college. In Sasha's own mind she knew that would be a big decision for her, but at least she had a choice is what she thought. Her father always told her to do what she had to do so that she would have a choice in life. He told her that many people who dropped out of school limited themselves from having choices in life, so in the end they just had to take what they could get. He told her if she put herself in a position where she could only take what she could get in life, she would surely be a miserable person.

Sasha looked at her watch and figured she'd take a ten-minute break. She went outside of the store and called Rebecca on the phone to tell her the news.

"Hey girl, I got a promotion today to become the new store manager, I'm so excited, but I am nervous because college is right around the corner and this is a long-term position that I can make a career of," said Sasha figuring she'd break the ice with the decision that had to be made before Rebecca chimed in on her.

"Wow, I am so proud of you Sasha. That's my best friend, that's my best friend," said Rebecca with excitement in her voice. "I'm so glad you are getting recognition for your dedication to that company."

"So, what would you do Rebecca, I really don't know what to think," asked Sasha?

"That is a great position to have Sasha, but we have both had our minds fixated on the sunshine state since we were in middle school," answered Rebecca as she remembered the day in middle school when her and Sasha made a pact to go to the sunshine state.

"You're right Rebecca and plus we are supposed to be making our own movie one day, I doubt that I could do that taking a career here. I'm glad I called you best friend, I'm going to tell Mr. Jackson now that I can't do it," said Sasha.

"No don't tell him yet, you just never know girl. Just think about it and maybe ask mom about it before you make the ultimate decision," replied Rebecca.

"You know what, you are right Rebecca. I'll pray on it," said Sasha.

"Well, on to the next subject. I think Nathan is about to propose to me. He got a promotion at the janitorial service today and thinks that he can handle whatever comes his way girl. You know our parents told us to go for the man with religion, employment and vision, and Nathan has all three. Since high school he has kept his same job and climbs as he goes, I'll just hate to leave him for UCLA, but if we're married, I hope he will come too," said Rebecca.

"I know that's right, girl. Nathan has been dedicated to you ever since the first day you two got together. You both deserve each other; I love you both and want the two of you to be happy. I don't know about myself, some man named Nick gave me his business card today and for some reason I have thought about calling him," said Sasha.

Rebecca listened to Sasha knowing she had heard that before from her, but no worthwhile results had ever come about. She really wanted her best friend to come out of her shell and knew she would before it was all said and done. Rebecca knew that Sasha was still hurt from Ronald but tried her best to help her move on from him and his memory as much as she could. She tried to tell Sasha all the time that she needed to open herself up and come out of her self-made prison, she also made it clear that Ronald wasn't the last man on earth.

"Well, we'll have to have a girl talk tonight Sasha. Talk to you later my boss is looking at me," said Rebecca as she hurried off the phone.

"Okay, bye," said Sasha as she hung up her phone.

Rebecca was the best friend you could ask for and so was Sasha. Through their years of knowing each other they never even had the least bit of an argument. Though their upbringings were very much different they still came together, and you could never tell the difference. Rebecca was one of six children with her being the only girl and the youngest child, while Sasha was the only child. Rebecca went without a lot of things growing up, but Sasha never went without anything. The way they smiled and enjoyed life you would have never thought either had a care in the world and that's what made them so close. After Sasha's father passed it was Rebecca who was the only person she could call on at times. For that reason and so many more Sasha knew in her heart she wouldn't stay in Indianapolis if Rebecca wasn't there with her.

Sasha wasn't even back in the store ten minutes before Drea stormed by her cussing and saying she was going on lunch break. Sasha being Sasha tried to calm her down. As soon as she got Drea to calm down she agreed to take a break with her. Sasha just looked around the store and every face seemed to be on her because everyone was happy, she calmed Drea down. This wasn't by far the first time an incident like this had occurred and like always it took Sasha to calm Drea down. Sasha then decided to take her lunch break instead of just another break and headed out with Drea.

Drea and Sasha approached the food court in Circle Centre Mall where they could find almost any food they could ask for. Both Sasha and Drea shared a common interest in Gyros, so they went straight to their normal place to dine. They shared small talk on the way to the counter. Everyone thought Drea was just hostile for no reason, but everything she did had reason behind it. She never went out starting trouble for no reason. Drea was just the type to handle whatever problem came to her in whichever way she seen fit to handle it.

"Sasha, them hoes in there are on my last nerves. Then they hate on you for no reason talking about you must be fucking Mr. Jackson. I put them hoes in check though," said Drea as Sasha tried to butt into her sentence but should have known not to because Drea always said what she had to say first.

"Drea, I'm not really worried about what they have to say. I've never been the type to fight evil with evil, I'd rather just leave it alone. Plus, I doubt that I'll take the position anyway, my SAT scores are coming soon so I might be going to UCLA," said Sasha as she went into her pocket fetching money to pay for her food.

A man walked up and stood in the back of them, but both girls let it blow off. Normally that would have been something to make Drea turn around swinging, but he didn't stand too close. They just continued with their conversation. Drea was super mad, but Sasha knew once she got her food she would calm down as she always did when she was mad, and food came into the picture. Drea and food had a very good relationship. Everyone always told Drea she could eat what she wanted because all her food seemed to digest in the right places. Even after having a child Drea still had the perfect body shape.

"Fuck that girl, you can't keep letting shit like that slide or you'll get ran over your whole life," Drea said as she got her money out of her pocket too.

"No ladies, I'll take care of your tabs for you," said the man who had walked up behind them.

Both ladies turned around to see who the man was trying to pay their tabs. Sasha looked and couldn't help, but to remember it was the guy from the store earlier that day and she did remember his name was Nick. Drea looked him up and down then put her hand on her hips. Drea had a look on her face that said, if he wants to pay then let him pay.

"Thank you, Nick, but I have my own money," said Sasha.

"It'll be my pleasure to pay for you beautiful ladies' to have lunch today, I just so happened to be in the mall still and seen you over here Sasha," said Nick.

Drea just stared at Nick the whole time like she knew him then said, "well, thank you Nick or whatever your name is I'm not about to argue with you about paying. Sasha let this nigga pay. I think I know you from somewhere though. Do you know me?"

"No, my dear, I don't know you, but it'll be a pleasure to buy you two ladies' lunch, Ms. Sasha," said Nick as he smiled at Sasha and then at Drea.

"Well, it's all good that you bought our food, but I still think I know you from somewhere. I'll let it go for now though," said Drea as she walked to the counter to pick both her and Sasha's food up. She then turned around and continued to say, "I guess I'll have to eat alone Sasha since Mr. Nick seems to be doing an X-Ray on your eyes with his eyes, you two can go have a seat. This must be the nigga who was in the store earlier."

Sasha laughed as her and Nick headed toward the tables to be seated, Drea went in the other direction still mumbling under her breath. Nick didn't have a bag in his hand nor anything else which seemed weird to Sasha, but she blew it off. As they approached a table Nick pulled out a chair and gestured for Sasha to have a seat, being a gentleman all the way. After she took her seat he went to the other side and sat down. Instead of going to a table to seat three or four, Nick chose the table to seat two meaning he wanted Drea to sit elsewhere anyway. As he began to take his seat, Drea was starting to walk up to them.

"Well, I guess I do have to eat alone since he picked out a table for two, but here's your food girl I have to call to make some appointments anyway. Mister whatever your name is don't get on no funny stuff with her because I'll be sitting right over there and I will remember where I know you from," said Drea, being funny in her own way as she gave Nick a dirty look. Drea walked away and Sasha could see Nick looking at Drea from the corner of his eyes, she didn't know if it was because of how her ass bounced in her work pants or something else.

"So, Ms. Sasha Williams, how is your day going, I couldn't help, but to try to catch you on lunch because I figured you would never use the business card I gave you," asked Nick as he looked at Sasha?

"My day is going fine, just trying to get done with it, you know," replied Sasha with a smile on her face. As she sat there in her seat being shy not wanting to eat in front of Nick.

"Well, you know you can eat in front of me," said Nick as they both laughed.

"I'm really not hungry, seems that I have to make many decisions today," said Sasha.

"I'm here to listen, give advice, or help you with whatever decisions you have to make. Being a business owner along with other things, decisions are something I must make many of daily. I'm here and all ears," replied Nick.

"I was told today that my current store manager is going to be leaving and going to another company and out of everyone he has chosen me to take his position after his departure. While it's a very good opportunity I'm determined to leave for college soon, so it's a big decision to make," Sasha said as she looked at Nick for an answer.

"Sasha, it's like this, you have to think about what you really want in life. While this could be a great opportunity at Nordstrom, it's also good to get your education so Nordstrom won't be your only option. Education opens up doors you would have never thought could be opened," said Nick.

For some reason, Sasha was impressed with the answer Nick had given her. She was really impressed to hear him talking about how education opens doors, which is something her dad would have told her. Sasha always told herself that if she was to be with any man, he would have to have characteristics like her father that she loved so much. She knew she would never find a man quite like her dad; however, a few characteristics was a big plus for her. Although she didn't know Nick, he did have her attention so far, so she wanted to get to know him a little bit more.

"Thanks a lot Nick, that really sounds like an answer my father would have answered with," said Sasha as she started to nibble at her food.

"I try my best Sasha. I've learned so much just by thinking things out before making an ultimate decision. By the way that's a great opportunity for you, it also explains a lot about your work ethics. I see you're very serious about your job and things like this shows that your hard work will pay off if you stay dedicated. Congratulations, but also think about it," said Nick.

"Aww, thanks Nick, but I want to know some things about you also. So, like my mother would say, what's your story," Sasha asked with a few giggles, but a serious look on her face?

Nick smiling with his pearly whites showing asked, "So where do you want me to start?"

"What do you do for a living? Do you have children? Do you have a girlfriend or wife? If you do have a girlfriend or wife then you shouldn't be talking to me that's just respect, I have for my fellow sisters," replied Sasha.

"Well, to start I don't have a woman, but I do socialize with a few women. I lost my wife to cancer five years ago, and just haven't had it in me to date again unless it's a woman like her," replied Nick.

Sasha interrupted, "I'm so sorry to hear that, I don't want you to have to think about it. Sorry for asking you this at this time."

Nick sat there with a sad look on his face while Sasha rubbed the top of his hand trying to console him.

Sasha could see the hurt in his eyes and felt bad for asking him about his deceased wife. It really wasn't her fault for asking, but Sasha was just that type of person. She had a very soft heart for other people feelings and never wanted to be the reason why anyone else felt pain.

"It's okay, you have no reason to apologize. We were married for seventeen years' and she has been gone five years. Now at the age of forty-one I just live my life through my work. I work sunup to sundown every day for my companies. I own real estate, two construction companies, a night club in Texas and mentor many men and youth. I try to stay busy in order to keep my mind in line with life and not think about sad times. I have a twenty-three-year-old daughter who stays in Nashville, Tennessee. Our relationship is good, but I wish it could be better," said Nick.

"Wow, I'm still sorry to hear that. I know how I feel about my dad and it gets very hard at times even though I know I have to live with it," said Sasha.

"It's a sad story, but it's on us to live out what our loved ones would have wanted us to live out. Yes, it's somewhat of a weakness, but also a strength at the same time. Seems that your dad had and has a big impact on your life which is a good thing, and I'm very sorry to hear that he's no longer here in the flesh with you, but know that he's here in spirit always," said Nick.

They both sat at the table with blank stares on their faces. Sasha broke the silence, and said, "you surely don't look forty-one."

"Thanks," said Nick with a smile on his face.

In Sasha's mind she knew, she was very impressed by Nick, but she would never let him know what she was thinking. She liked the fact that Nick was older and had things going for himself. Most of all she liked the fact that he had a demeanor like her father which she felt came from the fact that he was an older man. What she was very surprised about was the fact that she was interested in getting to know him, considering she threw so many men the cold shoulder daily. It was just something about Nick that caught her attention, she liked the feeling even though she didn't know him and had a lot more to learn about him.

"My pleasure," said Sasha as she started wrapping her food up. She went on to say, "my lunch will be over here shortly, and I still need to call my mother, so I think I'm going to leave for now."

"That's fine and I really enjoyed your company. Maybe next time we can do dinner or something like that, I mean if there is a next time," replied Nick with the look on his face like he was asking her out on a dinner date.

"That sounds nice. You can put my number in your phone and give me a call sometimes. I'm usually very busy, but there's nothing wrong with a text," said Sasha.

"Sounds good to me," said Nick as he pulled out one of his three phones.

Drea saw Sasha giving Nick her phone number and got up to approach the table they were eating at. By the time, she got to the table Sasha had already given Nick her phone number. Drea always called herself looking after Sasha and was very surprised to see her giving her number out. Out of all the time she had worked with Sasha, she seen men by the dozens try to holler at her, but never seen her show a lick of interest in any of them.

"Well, I see you two are getting acquainted. Mr. Nick don't be on no funny business with my friend, she's a very sweet girl and I will ride for her, you better believe that," said Drea with a calm voice, but with a serious look on her face.

"No need to worry young lady, I'm in everything I do for the long run. No funny business and no cutting corners," replied Nick.

"Yeah, okay that's what they all say. Just remember what I said, and I remember you like I said before I just can't pinpoint it right now," said Drea.

"Once you find out from where just let me know, you have a great day Sasha and stay beautiful," said Nick with a smile on his face as he got up to walk away.

"Thank you, sir, and you do the same," replied Sasha.

As the three parted ways Drea immediately said to Sasha, "Don't fall for no game from no man I don't care what kind of suit he wears or the cologne he has on. It's too much stuff going on out here and you have a great life ahead of you, I just want you to stay focused and not fall for anything stupid."

Sasha wondered why Drea was so protective over her, but she did like it because so far, she showed that she had nothing but love for her. Whenever there was a problem at work Drea was there for her. There was a lot of things Drea would take notice to that Sasha didn't even notice. It seemed that Drea knew everything about survival and taught Sasha something new every time they were at work. Drea just liked good people and had a heart for anyone she felt was naïve.

"I will keep you informed on everything Drea, thanks for always keeping my mind focused on the bigger picture of not getting played," said Sasha.

"No problem girl. I've seen so much in life and I've been through so much that I can't stand to see another home girl go through the same thing. I was once in your position and let a no-good fool impregnate me and now, I'm stuck doing everything for my son on my own," said Drea as she gave Sasha a serious look.

"Thanks girl, you're truly a blessing," answered Sasha as she put out her arms to give Drea a hug.

They hugged and went back to work. Sasha was called to the office several times to discuss her duties and confirm that she would take the position. As an intern, she would still have time to decide if she would permanently take the position or not, so she just told them she would see where things ended up. One thing about Sasha is that she was never in a rush to do anything and in this situation, she didn't want to cut herself short for a position that would take her away from living her dreams in the Sunshine state.

Sasha went back to her normal workday. She eventually went to the back of the store to call her best friend Rebecca back. She told Rebecca about her unexpected lunch with Nick and Rebecca was happy to hear the news but was still quiet about it because Sasha had tried going on dates before and found every reason to not go on another date with the same guy. Rebecca just thought to herself that a lot had happened for Sasha in just one day and they needed to talk.

CHAPTER 2

Sasha and Rebecca were sitting back having girl talk at Sasha's house when Sasha's phone began to ring. Normally Sasha's phone never really rang, especially at nighttime. Sometimes she felt like she paid a cellular phone bill for no reason. She had on her night clothes with her television set going like in her high school years. Her habits hadn't really changed. Only thing that was different in her life since high school was the fact that she wasn't in high school anymore. Looking at the strange number on her phone, Sasha answered, "hello."

"Hey there beautiful, this is Nick, hope I caught you at a good time!"

"Oh, hey there Nick, right now I'm kind of busy catching up with my best friend. Happy to hear from you, but can I give you a call back later," asked Sasha?

"Oh, yes that's fine, I'll be waiting on your call," answered Nick. Nick was ready to cuss her out because he didn't like her response but held his temper.

"Okay, I'll be sure to call you back," Sasha said with a bit of excitement in her voice.

Rebecca was looking at Sasha with a puzzled look on her face before asking, "Girl who was that, it sounded like I heard the voice of a man on your phone?"

"Girl that was a guy that came in the store a few weeks ago, the same one I had the unexpected lunch with. I almost thought he had forgotten about me. It's nothing though, just conversation," replied Sasha.

"Aww shoot now, my girl is getting back in the dating scene," said Rebecca as she got up and started to do a dance, "I told you that you have to open yourself up again, we are both still young and have too much life ahead of us to stay bottled up, Sasha."

Sasha laughed and said, "no Rebecca, this is just a nice guy I met while I was working, who actually came out of nowhere and bought lunch for a coworker and myself."

"So, he must have just guessed your number then," asked Rebecca in a joking manner?

"Girl stop it, but he does seem like a nice guy and he's very attractive, so I might just go on a date with him, he has already offered," said Sasha.

"That's what I'm talking about girl," said Rebecca as she went for a high five with Sasha.

"Now tell me what you know about him girl," said Rebecca as she sat Indian style on Sasha's bed giving her all her attention.

"Well, I don't know much, but I do know he's a business owner and a well-mannered man," replied Sasha.

"Okay, I guess you'll figure the rest of it out when he takes you on a date," said Rebecca.

"Yeah, I guess," said Sasha as they both laughed.

"So, do you like the position so far Sasha," asked Rebecca?

"Yes, it's a great position, but I just know in my heart I don't want to take it. I mean everything is there, it just seems like I'll be missing out on something if I just take the position and not see what an education from UCLA has to offer," replied Sasha.

"Sasha, you know I would hate to go to UCLA alone, but I want you to only think about what's best for you in this situation. While it may seem like you're settling if you take this position you're not. You must keep in mind that there are many people in college as we speak that have their minds set on having this very position. So, think about that Sasha. Make a conscious decision and I mean it Sasha," said Rebecca.

"I understand what you're saying, and I have somewhat thought about it, but I guess it's just still fresh on me. If I were to take it, I do like the fact that I wouldn't have to leave momma behind because I do know I would miss her. Momma keeps telling me to follow my heart like you're saying. I really don't know Rebecca," said Sasha as she started to look depressed.

"Your decision will come soon enough girl. Just keep your fingers crossed and pray for the best outcome on whatever choice you make, I'm rocking with you regardless, cheer up girl," said Rebecca.

As the night went on the girls just sat back and talked about old times that brought much joy to their lives. Neither of the girls had a clue about life really, but Rebecca had many examples as she was the youngest of her siblings and seen her parents and brothers go through a lot in life. They were two young ladies who just wanted the best out of life and had each other's back no matter what. Rebecca was sexually active and in love with Nathan, while Sasha was a virgin and heart broken. In a way, Rebecca was more at peace in life, while Sasha was still trying to figure everything out in all aspects of life. The good thing about the two is that they learned from each other and no matter what, they always came to each other when it was time to make decisions.

In their middle school years, they built an unbreakable bond. A bond that many classmates tried to come between. Guys in school would clown them all the time because they didn't want to give them the time of day. They were made fun of, laughed at and considered nerds in school most of their years. The thing was that Rebecca could fight well and once she was pushed to the limit she would strike. Sasha did have a few fights in school that she won, but she would cry herself to sleep at night every time she was in a fight. Neither of them wanted any trouble, but Rebecca would step up to fight before Sasha would.

Rebecca was having problems at home in high school and moved in with Sasha and her parents for her whole sophomore year of high school. When it was time to move back home neither of them wanted to depart from the same house. Rebecca did move out on her own as soon as she turned eighteen, but Sasha was just a momma's girl who never wanted to leave home. She could have left on many occasions and had the money to move, but never did. She really didn't want to leave to go to UCLA, but knew she had to grow up sooner than later.

"Well, best friend I'm a go ahead and get out of here, I have to meet Nathan at the gym. I would ask you if you were coming, but you have been so busy at work that I know you're not up to it. Since you would never miss a day before and now you've missed many," said Rebecca as she pushed Sasha on the thigh.

"I know right, I have to get back into the spirit of working out. I see myself adding on a few pounds," Sasha said as she stood up and looked in her full body view mirror.

"Girl, you still got the body that many women go to the gym to try to achieve daily. Believe me you're okay," replied Rebecca as she stood up next to Sasha and gave her a high five.

"You always say the right things Rebecca, I love you, now go to the gym girl before Nathan start calling," said Sasha looking at Rebecca with her eyes squinted.

After Sasha gave her a hug and Rebecca told her she loved her in return, Rebecca headed out. Sasha did a few things around the house and upheld her promise to call Nick back. Nick answered the phone and their conversation was nonstop. They talked on just about every level. Sasha didn't talk on the phone much so staying on the phone for the hours they had been talking meant he caught her interest. He informed her that he was raised in church and lived by the principles of the bible and that really made Sasha give the thumbs up in her mind. By the end of the conversation the two planned a date for a later time that week. Sasha was all smiles and it felt good to her that she could smile considering all the stress she had faced over the past few weeks. So far, so good, is what she thought.

When Sasha broke the news to her mother, Rebecca and Drea that she was going on a date they all were happy she was starting to do something different.

Drea still had to put her two cents in it telling her to watch her back and to call her if she needed her. Rebecca kind of felt bad because she felt like she had forced Sasha into dating again. When Rebecca told Sasha how she felt, Sasha reminded her that she was only doing what a friend was supposed to do. Sasha's mother did what any mother would do and questioned her to the fullest about who she was going on a date with. Her mother also told her that she wanted to meet him before he took her daughter anywhere, like Sasha was still a teenager.

After Sasha and Nick's first date they were pretty much inseparable. Nick went to pick her up in a new Porsche. He did feel kind of odd having to meet her mother before the first date like they were still in school, but just kept that thought to himself. He was surprised by the beauty of Sasha's mother and complimented her multiple times. He took Sasha out to eat her favorite food, which was Mexican food. He took her to a place called Cancun Mexican Restaurant,

located in a suburb outside Indianapolis, called Carmel.
Carmel is where many rich people stayed at to have
peace.

He really treated her good on their first date.
Never did he try to make any advances on her at all.
Anything she asked about on the menu he bought for
her, even though she told him not to. He told her that
she would never know what her favorite was if she
didn't try things. He ordered the Fajita Nachos for
himself, which was his favorite. He was a big man, so
he had extra steak, chicken and shrimp in his nachos.
Sasha laughed at him because she didn't know how he
could eat so much. She had many different entrées and
just ate a little of each and took the rest home. Nick had
a Margarita, but Sasha didn't drink, so she denied the
offer. That was Sasha's first time at Cancun, and she
loved it.

Nick showered Sasha with flowers at work. He
sent lunch to her every day from the most expensive
restaurants in Indianapolis. Places that didn't even

deliver still delivered for Nick somehow. Sasha was very happy and satisfied with Nick. Everyone at her job thought surely Sasha had sex with Nick, but the truth was that she hadn't, and they had never even discussed sex. Drea was always telling Sasha how happy she was for her and in the same breath telling her to watch herself. Rebecca was very happy for Sasha and the two of them along with Nick and Nathan double dated on more than one occasion. If you'd have seen Sasha and Nick in public, you'd have thought they had already been together for years. The way they embraced and looked at each other only defined love.

Over the next couple months Sasha had matured into her new position, got a raise and found love. She was at the point where she was going to stay with Nordstrom and delete UCLA from her agenda. Rebecca could tell Sasha was comfortable with her new life and wouldn't try to persuade Sasha to do anything she didn't think to do for herself, she just wanted Sasha to be happy. Sasha's date was coming up to give corporate her ultimate decision on if she was going to take the position permanently or not. Many managers from corporate came to the store to personally thank Sasha for her service and let her know that sales had went up tremendously at her store location. The sales went up so much that she was getting unexpected bonus after unexpected bonus. Sasha learned a lot from Nick when it came to business and he sure didn't mind teaching her.

Everyone had seen a big change in Sasha. Even the women at work who once talked about her now looked up to her and was happy for her. Sasha's mother was very proud of her daughter and complimented her every day. Her mother wanted her to keep on the path she was on because she knew it was the only way Sasha would learn to still be happy after her father passed. Sasha still thought about her father every day but could still smile and use what he taught her in life, which she didn't have the strength to do at first. If you were on the outside looking in you would have saw Sasha as the happiest woman walking the earth and, in her mind, she was.

Rebecca was her normal self over the months just getting ready for UCLA. Her and Nathan were even closer than before. She just knew in her heart he would be proposing to her soon. In the back of her mind she also knew he would be going to California with her when she left for college, that was what she hoped for every day. After all, she knew Sasha had everything she needed in Indianapolis so her chances of going to UCLA were slim to none. If Sasha was happy then Rebecca was happy no matter what. Rebecca knew secrets about Sasha's insecurities and no one else on earth knew these things about Sasha. It seemed to her that Sasha was slowly coming out of her shell for Nick, which was a good thing because in Rebecca's eyes Nick was a good man and a good fit for Sasha. Though Rebecca didn't like that Nick was so much older than Sasha. She just let it ride as a "whatever makes her happy" statement.

Sasha's mother felt Sasha was going to be leaving her soon either to go to UCLA or to get her own place and she really didn't like the feeling. Sasha had been in the same house as her all her life and the feeling of her leaving left a feeling of emptiness in her mother's heart. She really dreaded the day that Sasha would leave home but knew it would come sooner than later. Although her mother never showed it, she was still feeling empty inside without her husband. To lose Sasha too was just way too much, but she knew she had to hold it together.

Drea and Sasha had started to build an even closer bond after Sasha's promotion. Sasha gave Drea a promotion to become the manager of the make-up department. Drea was a cosmetologist and make-up artist so she was very happy with her position. After Drea's promotion make-up sales went up by at least thirty percent which made corporate very happy. Drea was in a better position in life and could only thank Sasha. Drea also picked up a lot of side money doing hair for the many customer's that came to Nordstrom. She was a single mother and now could provide for her son the way she always wanted to so nobody could tell her nothing. She even went and purchased a new car and it was the car she always wanted, a brand-new black on black Chevy Impala. Drea always tried to talk Sasha into upgrading from her high school car which was an old school four door Regal. Sasha never gave in though, even though her Regal was a little beat up she still loved her car. Plus, material things didn't really impress Sasha, she got her old fashion ways from her father, she looked at the purpose of whatever it was and if it served its purpose, she was happy. The restaurants, gifts and lifestyle that Nick exposed Sasha to was new to her and kind of excited her, but she stayed her normal self.

Nick purchased Sasha many things over their time of dating. One of Sasha's favorite items Nick had bought her was a Carolina Herrera dress. He even bought her burgundy Valentino stilettos to match. Sasha almost fainted when she seen the receipt for the purchase of the dress and heels. She seen he had spent over six thousand dollars on just those two items and tried to get him to take it back, but as always Nick told her she deserved the best of the best and it was his pleasure. Though Sasha had never gone without, she still never had gifts showered on her like that, especially with such high price tags on them. It would be hard for Sasha to adapt to such a high-end lifestyle and she really didn't want to, but Nick just kept on showering her. Nick took Sasha to the Lexus dealer to purchase her a brand-new Lexus, but Sasha firmly refused a car. Nick did get Sasha to promise that she would consider a new car before long though, but at that moment a car was just too much for Sasha to accept. All the other gifts were forced on her because he would just purchase them and drop them off to her.

Drea warned Sasha that men who usually did things like Nick had been doing for her usually had something to cover up, but in Sasha's mind that was just Drea speaking her mind. Plus, sometimes Drea could go way overboard with theories so Sasha just let it bypass her. On top of that Drea could never tell Sasha where she knew Nick from but kept saying she knew him from somewhere and that made Sasha kind of look at Drea like she was a schizophrenic. Sasha still respected Drea and loved her the same, she just overlooked a lot of what Drea had to say. Not only that Nick told Sasha that she needed to start living her own life and quit worrying about other people opinions and she felt where he was coming from.

One day Sasha's mother did want to have a talk with her about Nick. She seen him buy her so many things that she thought Sasha had to have had sex with him. Sasha promised her mother she didn't, and her mother told her that she was grown, but if anything, she just wanted Sasha to use protection. What many didn't know is that the thought of sex made Sasha sick to her stomach. She watched a few porn videos with her ex Ronald and just didn't see what all the hype was about.

Nick even bought things for Sasha's mother, Rebecca, and gave Nathan many odd jobs to make money. Nathan really needed extra money and Nick gave him the opportunities because Nathan told him that he wanted to propose to Rebecca in an extravagant way. Nick could feel Nathan on wanting to be extravagant, so he helped him out. Everybody liked Nick and what made them like him even more was his love for Sasha. They always went out to eat and to the movies. They cooked at Sasha's home, played cards and watched movies. Nick came in and made himself a part of the family and he constantly thanked them because it had been a while since he had a family life. Ever since his wife died and his daughter moved out of state, he never really had closeness with anyone, so he really enjoyed Sasha and all her people. They all felt bad for Nick because of his loss, they wanted him to feel at home with them, and let him know that he did have people who cared about him.

Sasha's ex-boyfriend thought Sasha would never move on and once he found out about Nick, he was very angry. Ronald tried everything he could to get back into Sasha's life. He went to her job, sent flowers to her job and even went to her house. Ronald went to Sasha's mother and she told Ronald that she would always look at him like a son, but she doubted that it would ever be a chance for him to be with Sasha again. Nick eventually had to go to Ronald and ask him to quit harassing Sasha. After Nick's talk with Ronald, Ronald just stayed his distance. No one knew what Nick said to him, but they knew it worked and Sasha was happy it worked.

Nick was happy himself that Ronald stayed away after his talk with him. Nick didn't want to resort to violence but knew he would if he had to. He made a promise to himself that he would protect Sasha, even if it was with his own life, he just wanted her to be safe. He was thinking in his mind that he wanted Sasha to be his wife, he just didn't know how she would take it if he asked her. Since he had taken Sasha to every place in Indianapolis worth going to, he told her to take a vacation from work, so he could take her somewhere nice. He also told Sasha to ask her mother, Rebecca, and Nathan if they wanted to come along as well. When she told him, no one could afford to take a vacation from work, he laughed at her and with a serious face told her to ask them.

<u>CHAPTER 3</u>

Nick and Nathan woke up before everyone and creeped out the condo Nick rented for them all on their vacation. Nick somewhat forced them into their Miami, Florida vacation but they didn't have not one complaint. Sasha, her mom, and Rebecca were still sound asleep. Nick rented them one condo and slept in his bed alone, since him and Sasha weren't sexually active and out of respect for her mother, he told her it would only be right for her to share a room with her mother. Nick's respect for Sasha and everyone she knew made her even more head over hills for him. The fellas were headed to Fontana's to get breakfast so they could surprise the ladies with breakfast in bed. Nick was very familiar with Miami and had just sold his vacation home located there a few months earlier. Nick and Nathan chose Fontana's after Nick told Nathan how good their Belgian waffles were. They both knew this breakfast in bed would make the ladies day, especially after they drove for hours on the highway to get to

Miami the day before. They chose to drive because Sasha's mother was scared to get on an airplane, she told them to just enjoy themselves, but Nick insisted that they drive so she could join them.

While in the restaurant they ordered everyone their favorite breakfast food and a lot of extra entrées too so they could all try them. Both fellas had smiles on their faces just knowing this would make the women happy plus surprise them at the same time. Nathan loved this idea presented to him by Nick. Nathan was a good guy and was a young man still trying to learn how to treat a woman. Nick knew he was still young and loved Nathan's drive to always reach for more and, he could just see himself all over again at Nathan's age. Even though when Nick was Nathan's age, he had his own paper route service delivering the Indianapolis Star Newspaper for the City of Indianapolis, with a dozen drivers driving for him.

Rebecca woke up before the other ladies and panicked when she didn't see Nathan. She immediately called his phone. She was used to waking up to hearing Nathan snoring every morning. So, when she woke up in an unfamiliar place without him there, she felt odd. She doubted that anything was wrong, but still wanted to check on him.

"Hey, are you okay," asked Rebecca?

"Yes, I'm fine. Just took a little spin with Nick for a few. We will be back after a while, go on back to sleep honey," replied Nathan as he quickly finished his conversation with her. After hanging up the phone Nathan looked at Nick with a confused expression on his face.

Both fellas wanted breakfast in bed to be a surprise to the ladies, so Nathan couldn't tell her the secret about them being at the restaurant. Nathan had never lied to Rebecca and felt he lied to her just because he wasn't all the way honest, plus he didn't like that he rushed her off the phone. Nick assured him that he didn't lie, they did take a spin, so he was telling the truth. What Nick said made perfect sense to Nathan, so he let it blow off his mind. Nick also let him know that as a man, he had to keep somethings to himself. He told him there were some things men didn't share with their women, just like women had things they didn't share with their men.

Nathan felt a sense of relief that Rebecca did sound like she was going back to sleep. He told Nick that Rebecca was going back to sleep, so Nick felt relief as well. The fellas order came, and they headed for the Condo. Once they entered the Condo, they went straight in the kitchen to prepare the meals on ceramic plates, and the plates would sit on gold trays lined with diamonds. In no way was this going to be a simple prepared breakfast. Nick had put a lot of thought into this whole trip even the simple details had much thought put into them. Nick was just that type of guy, if he was to do anything it was always going to be big.

The women woke up to knocks on the door and the repeated words of, "room service" from the guys. Nathan had Rebecca's meal on the tray and Nick had

Sasha and her mother's meals on trays, though he had to carry them one at a time, which he treated her mother first out of respect. Sasha woke up and said, "come in" first and Rebecca soon after said the same thing.

"Hey, sweetie, this is your mother's, I'm about to get yours now," said Nick as he pulled out the legs of the tray and set it up for her mother to eat.

Sasha's mother woke up and had a smile that made her whole face light up. What no one else knew is that it reminded her of her husband doing the same for her while he was alive. Though she was happy, she was still kind of sad at the same time. She didn't show it, but that's what she felt. She thanked Nick even when he was in the kitchen going to fetch his and Sasha's trays, which he grabbed both since he didn't have to reach down and grab the door handle this time. He came back in the room and set up Sasha's tray for her. Then went to open the blinds to see the only thing you could see which was a beautiful view of sand, water, and waves a short distance away. There was also a couch and table set up in the room Sasha and her mother occupied, which is where Nick was attempting to sit before, he was interrupted by a hug from Sasha.

"Baby, thank you so much," said Sasha as she kissed Nick on the lips.

"Anything I can do to make you smile, I will do sweetie," said Nick as he hugged Sasha with a strong hold.

Sasha's mom just looked at them in awe, she was very happy for them. It was like right out the clear blue-sky things had gotten better for her daughter and she loved it. She always wanted her daughter to be happy, so she had no complaints. Her mother didn't care much about the gifts and things like that, what she cared about was her daughter being happy. Sasha's mom was in her mid-forties and still looked very good herself, but as a widow she stayed to herself. Nick was nearly her age and that was a concern to her at first, but if he made her daughter happy, she didn't care if he would have happened to be older than her. Sasha's mother's name was Tammy, but her nickname was "Tam the dream" growing up because it was a dream for men to be with her. She never gave them the time of day, so they all called her a dream and named her "Tam the dream."

Meanwhile Rebecca was so pleased with the breakfast her and Nathan had eaten. That she opened the blinds and made love to Nathan as the glare from the sun beamed on them. They were so in love that they could never keep their hands off each other. No one knew it was Nick's idea about breakfast in bed and he wanted to keep it that way because it was Nick's way of showing him a way to please a woman. Rebecca could see the change in Nathan and she really loved the change, not that she wasn't happy at first in any way. It just seemed to Rebecca that Nathan was maturing even more with Nick around. She knew Nathan's father was killed when Nathan was in middle school and liked the fact, he had a positive male role model in his life now.

As the day went on, they went to many fascinating places in Miami. Nick directed them to all the places they went to, considering he was the only one who had been to Miami before. He was still having the time of his life like everyone else because he felt he was with great people. He rode them around to so many places, they sampled an abundance of great foods from many great restaurant's and went to the mall to buy souvenirs along with other small items. He even took them to tour his old house in Miami, which they were all knocked off their feet by the beauty of the place.

As the day was starting to turn to night, he told them he had a place he wanted them to eat dinner at. He planned to take them to a Japanese restaurant called Zuma. He chose Zuma because of their delicious food and the great scenery that came with it. He also knew that Sasha had never had Japanese food before and wanted to give her an opportunity to try something new. Every one of them was ready for dinner and excited to try the restaurant out since Nick bragged on it so much.

What the crowd didn't know was that Nick had reserved them a section in Zuma, where they would be treated like stars.

They got to the restaurant and were all pleased with the place. It was something they had never experienced in Indianapolis. No one really knew what to order so Nick told them to just order a variety of foods to see what things tasted like as he always said. Nick was really being a gentleman on this night like he always did. Sasha's mother was totally blown away with the adventures Nick had taken them on, and the restaurant just put her over the top. They all sat around the table eating, talking and enjoying themselves. Nick and Tammy were the only ones who had cocktails, since Sasha, Rebecca or Nathan didn't drink. The waiter treated them like they were a royal family. Everyone who worked there knew Nick and knew that whenever he came, he tipped very generously, they knew he was a very respectful and respected man.

There were so many different dishes of food on the table that no one knew where to begin. If you were on the outside looking in, you'd have thought a hungry football team was about to eat. They all took turns telling stories about the most embarrassing moments in their lives. It was all fun and games. They talked about what they would be if each of them had to become an animal. The topic changed many times as they all laughed at one another.

Sasha's mind was all over the place. She wondered what she had done so good to deserve so good of treatment from Nick. Drea stayed in contact with her every moment of the way. Nick told Sasha that she should have just asked Drea if she wanted to come along. Nick was serious about asking her if she wanted to come, but in a way, he was trying to tell Sasha to quit focusing on her phone and focus on him. It was a headache to have Drea calling just about every half hour. That was just Drea though, wanting to know every detail along the way.

As dinner came to an end, Nick told everyone to order a dessert of their choice. They told him they were fine, but he insisted on everyone ordering dessert. So, everyone ordered. They sat there and chatted until dessert was brought to the table. When the waiter came with dessert, dessert was on plates with dome type lids on them, everything was gold. The waiter put everyone's dessert in front of them first then started to take off everyone's lid which Sasha was the last one to have her lid taken off. When the waiter did take Sasha's lid off there was a three-carat platinum diamond ring in it instead of dessert, with the words "will you marry me" written in chocolate on the plate.

Nick then dropped down to one knee while grabbing the ring off the plate avoiding the chocolate that surrounded the ring. Nicks words were, "Sasha, I know this may be soon for you, but I know what I want, need, and ask for in life and that's a woman like you. Will You Marry Me?" When he said that, everyone at the table looked lost.

At that time, everyone in the restaurant jumped to their feet and started to clap for them. The music changed to a Jesse Powell song called "You." Sasha and the rest of the bunch were lost for words and that's when tears came from Sasha's eyes and she said, "Yes." He put the ring on her finger which glistened in the light like it was the light itself. Then he stood up and offered her to dance to the song. They danced while everyone in the restaurant said their congratulations and cheered them on. Tammy, Rebecca and Nathan all sat there in awe; they were very happy for Sasha. As this was the most incredible thing any of them had ever seen in life. Even Sasha's mother was in shock as she had never seen anything like this in her life, she thought it was very creative. She knew Nick would propose but didn't know when and where he would do it. Nick had gone to Sasha's mother days earlier to ask if she would accept him if he was to propose to Sasha and she said yes. Nick asked Sasha's mother out of respect, since her father had died, he figured it would only be right to ask her mother.

Although Zuma was a restaurant, you would have never known by the way everyone got up and started to dance. It was a perfect night and any woman would have felt special after such a night. Many other couples were having dinner in the restaurant and went to show their respect to the newly engaged couple. Sasha even had a drink herself that night, after many people in the restaurant sent drinks to their table. Though Sasha only had a shot, she was still feeling a little buzzed considering it was her first drink ever. Just when everyone was thinking the night couldn't have gotten any better, the manager came over to tell them that all their meals were on the house. Nick had spent so much money at Zuma in the past that when the waiter told the manager he proposed there, the manager said to put everything on the house and told him not to accept a tip from Nick.

After sitting around for a while, the group decided to head back out to the condo. To their surprise, Nick had another surprise up his sleeve. After stepping out of the restaurant the group was met by a party bus big enough to seat at least thirty people. The bus had a full bar, Jacuzzi tub, and plush white leather furniture. Televisions surrounded the bus, everything was white and gold, even the televisions were gold. That's when Nick informed them that they would cruise the city of Miami for the night. Then they would head to Orlando for Disney World the next morning. Though Disney World was usually an attraction for children, Nick wanted to take Sasha because she told him she always wanted to go as a child, but never went.

So far, the crew had the time of their lives and there was still more in store. Nick just knew in his mind he would make Sasha the happiest woman living. He had no limits when it came to her. In his life, he had made a lot of money and was very generous when it came time to spend it. Nick had tried to date a few women, but most of them were out for his pockets and once he figured that out, he would kick them to the curb quickly. Nick despised those who looked for handouts. For some reason, Nick was always that way, even when it came to his family. With Sasha, it was just something different. She never asked him for anything at all and really the simplest things in life made her happy. This was something new for Nick, but he still forced things on her because he loved the finer things. They rode in the party bus until the wee hours of the morning and slept the whole way to Disney World. At Disney World, they all enjoyed themselves like they were children again. By the time, it was time to go, no one wanted to leave.

CHAPTER 4

After arriving back to Indianapolis, Sasha started to plan her wedding. Nick told her however she wanted to do the wedding was totally up to her, all that mattered to him was that she was happy. Instead of Sasha planning a big wedding, she chose a smaller one. Sasha chose to have her wedding at her families' church, Eastside Seventh Day Adventist. She planned to have their reception at the Madame CJ Walker theater in downtown Indianapolis. Sasha left the honeymoon up to Nick as he requested. The wedding was just two weeks away and would be the biggest day of Sasha's life and she had no doubts that every day after she would still feel the same way.

Nick informed Sasha that she would no longer have to work after they were to tie the knot. After all she would be part owner of his multi-million-dollar enterprise. Nick told her she could do things the way she wanted to do them in their enterprise. Sasha told Rebecca about what Nick told her and even Rebecca changed her mind about going to college in California, instead she would take a good paying position in the enterprise also. Nick had already abducted Nathan into the enterprise, so it would be all of them working hard for the same cause. Nick ran the same enterprise for over ten years and the growth was outstanding, so no one had doubts after seeing the timeline of growth and the vision for the future. Nick informed Sasha that he wanted to keep their circle small and that everyone she hired within their circle would receive a sign on bonus of twenty-five thousand dollars, which they would get a check at the time of their signing. For these young adults, full of energy, this was a dream come true.

Sasha gave Nordstrom a two-week notice, which upset corporate highly, but they were still happy for her. Drea would take over the store after Sasha was to depart. Sasha gave a good word for Drea and that's what landed her the spot. Drea was happy for Sasha and herself at the same time. Drea knew all the ins and outs of the store operations because of Sasha. Plus, Drea had also put up big numbers for Nordstrom in her department, so everything for the future looked promising for all parties. Drea told Sasha thanks, but still warned her to watch out for snakes though she didn't say Nick's name, Sasha knew what she was hinting around to.

While Sasha was handling all the business she needed to handle with work and the wedding, Nick was handling the enterprise and the honeymoon arrangements. With their big day coming up soon, they were both busy. Sasha did think about if she was moving too fast or not after listening to Drea, but really, she had no doubts, so she just kept on with her planning. After all her mother told her that time had nothing to do with love, and sometimes too much thought into things could mess up good things. Sasha wasn't impressed by Nick's money at all, she just loved the way he treated her. She remembered her grandmother telling her about her and her grandfather's marriage starting only three weeks after they met and that lasted until death did them apart. So, Sasha just rolled with the punches and was ready to take Nick in as her husband.

In the days leading up to their wedding they were talked about all over Indianapolis in a good and bad way. Sasha was popular in the Indianapolis world somewhat, but not as popular as Nick, as Nick knew people from all over, Sasha was secluded to a small few. They both received dirty looks wherever they went, but they both just brushed it off. By Nick's name being so popular in the whole city of Indianapolis. Many women wanted to be with him and were envious of Sasha once they found out about him proposing to her. No matter what others tried to do to break off the marriage, nothing worked to their benefit. Sasha and Nick both found what they longed for in life and weren't going to let no one destroy what they were building.

When their wedding day came around, they filled up Eastside Seventh Day Adventist Church. Many people came from out of town. Sasha came down the aisle in an all-white Berta open back beaded lace corset dress, with platinum Sergio Rossi heels lined in diamonds. Nick was dressed in a platinum Brunello Cucinelli tuxedo suit, with platinum diamond spiked Christian Louboutin loafers on his feet. Though they chose to have a small wedding, they did go all out for every other feature involved in their wedding. Anyone who knew Nick knew he was known for an expensive taste when it came to clothes especially. They looked very good at their wedding. They hired a professional photographer who snapped pictures from every angle. Their decorations looked like something straight out of a magazine. To anyone who didn't know them, they were a famous couple by the way their wedding arrangements were set up. Nick even went as far as to buy a sixty thousand-dollar red Persian Tabriz wool rug for Sasha to walk down the aisle on. As she walked down the aisle, a Jagged Edge song, called "Promise," played from the interior speakers of the church. To say they did it big for their wedding would be an understatement, especially coming from Indianapolis as normal citizens. As they exchanged vows, you could see the tears come from Sasha's eyes. Nick stood there with a look of satisfaction on his face as he grinned. Both sides of the aisles were filled with joy for the two. Thousands of pictures were taken, and many gifts were given from the guests. This was a wedding that was going to be remembered.

As the wedding ended Nick walked Sasha down the aisle to exit the church. To her surprise, he had another surprise up his sleeve. Nick had her three vehicles as her wedding gifts. He bought her a brand-new Range Rover, a brand-new convertible Corvette and an old school 1972 Chevy Chevelle convertible. All of them were pink with platinum graphics, with the convertibles having platinum tops to match the graphics. He put the Range Rover on thirty-inch Forgiato rims for her, the convertibles both were sitting on twenty-eight-inch Forgiato rims, and all the rims were the same design. Nick had really gone all out for his wife and she loved every minute of it. She wasn't used to these types of things nor knew what they were for that matter, she did love the beauty of the vehicles though. As this was all new to her, she just took things as they came.

She couldn't help, but to hug Nick after such a big surprise. He had a bow tied around each vehicle. All the attendees at the wedding were in total shock. They went up to examine the vehicles and the Chevelle just stood out like a sore thumb. Everything in it was redone and even had a chrome engine. Nick had twenty-three TV's installed in it and invested over twenty-five-thousand-dollars in the stereo system. There was plush platinum and gray interior with the pink piping. All three were dream cars and in no way, were they normal, they all had custom paint, interior and rims. Sasha was ready to jump in the Chevelle to drive off to the reception, but just as she made a step towards it, a stretch Hummer pulled up with just married signs on it. Nick looked at Sasha with a smile on his face.

"Sweetie, I wouldn't be a man in my eyes if my wife had to drive on her wedding day," said Nick as he put his hand out for Sasha to grab.

"Nick, you always leave me speechless, thanks baby," said Sasha.

Sasha, Nick and many others loaded into the Hummer, heading to the reception. All three of Sasha's new vehicles followed the stretch Hummer as the drivers blew the horns. Nick already had drivers set up to drive all of Sasha's vehicles to the reception. Sasha really did make Nick feel better about himself. Nick for once in life felt like he completed a woman and that gave him a satisfaction he never had before. Nick just wanted a woman to enjoy his life with and he had that with Sasha, and to his benefit she was still a virgin. He sat in the back of the Hummer next to his wife feeling like he was on top of the world, and the feeling came because of Sasha, not because the Hummer was sitting high on thirty-six-inch rims. The whole ride to the reception was filled with laughter and memorable moments with the photographer inside still snapping pictures.

Before they headed to the reception, they stopped at the Indiana Art Museum to take their outside wedding pictures. Nick, Sasha and everyone who was a part of their wedding was in the pictures. Nick being Nick he just had to take pictures in front of Sasha's new cars along with the other pictures. He wanted every part of their wedding to be in a picture so they could always look back in the years to come. They had many different beautiful backgrounds at the Art Museum to take pictures in front of and they took advantage of them all.

After leaving the Art Museum they headed downtown to take pictures on the Canal and on what they call Monument Circle in Indianapolis. All views were gorgeous, with waterfalls and everything. Nick hired one of the best photographers in the United States to take their pictures. He hired him because he didn't want there to be any mistakes when it came to their wedding pictures. While they were leaving downtown to head to the reception, Nick popped a bottle of champagne in the Hummer and cranked up the music. The party got started before they even got to the reception.

They all walked into the reception ready to party the night away, though Sasha and Nick had to have an early night due to their early flight in the morning for their honeymoon. Nick didn't want the party to end for everyone because they would have to leave early, so he paid to have the building all night in advance. The room was set up in an extravagant way, it was all white everything. So much food filled the serving tables that you couldn't even see the tables. They even went as far as to have foods from different countries flown in, just to give everyone a taste of different foods from all over the world. They had one hundred and fifty bottles of wine in different flavors and brands. They had a wide selection of liquor when it came to hard liquor. They went all out and made it enjoyable for everyone. Their wedding cake stood high like a tower; the actual height of the cake was the same height as Sasha.

Drea was very impressed herself. Sasha told her they would have a small wedding, but in Drea's eyes the wedding nor the reception was small at all. She figured at least a half of million dollars was spent on this wedding. She knew that Nick was wealthy, but she wondered why he was going all out like he was doing. By this time, she figured she would keep her thoughts to herself. After all Nick was Sasha's husband now and if he made Sasha happy then what could she say.

Everyone went to get their plates and while in line, Nick came with another surprise. Keith Sweat to everyone's surprise came through the door singing, "Right and Wrong Way." This took the crowd by surprise, many of the women looked like they were about to faint. Others just sang along with the song. Nick reached for Sasha so they could dance. Everyone who was about to eat changed their direction and headed to the dance floor. There were so many flashes from cameras that you didn't even need a fluorescent light on to keep the room lit. Sasha's mother got up to dance to one of her favorite songs by Keith Sweat as well. Nick had everything in line and didn't care about the price when it came to him making the day special for his wife. Keith Sweat sang many of his greatest songs. Everyone ate good, danced good, and drank good. Everything went according to plan in Nick's eyes and he loved when things went the way they were supposed to go.

Nick and Sasha stayed and partied for as long as they could. Sasha had never really danced in her whole life, but Nick made sure she knew some moves before the time they left their reception. At first Sasha felt embarrassed, but after seeing how much fun it looked like Nick was having, she eased up. She played a few songs for Nick before the night was out. One song she played was a Faith Evans song called, "Never Let You

Go." They danced and danced like they didn't have a worry in the world. Before leaving Sasha cut the cake and everyone at the reception indulged.

The next morning the newly wedded couple were on a flight heading to Miami, Florida. When they got to Florida they went to the beach and to Sasha's surprise there was another surprise. Nick had rented a Submarine Superyacht for them to cruise the bottom of the ocean in, for their honeymoon. The submarine was filled with everything you could possibly think of. It was literally a mansion that went under water, equipped with nine bedrooms, four bathrooms, two kitchens, an electric fireplace and more. Sasha didn't know what to say, as always, she was lost for words. Everything in the submarine was of an expensive taste, it even had Leonardo Da Vinci paintings hanging from the ceiling. The submarine was as romantic as it could get, plus more. On top of that it was something different even for Nick himself, which he wanted to do something new for them both. They would occupy the submarine for seven days and after that he had another seven days booked for them in Cancun, Mexico.

As they cruised the bottom of the ocean, they laid back in the bed talking and laughing about conversations on all sorts of topics. That's when Nick turned to Sasha and began to kiss her. Sasha knew her virginity was about to be taken and for once in life she didn't mind her virginity ending. He slowly took off all her clothes and got up to remove his own. As he climbed back in the bed filled with rose peddles, he climbed in from the bottom of the luxurious bed. He started licking and sucking on Sasha's toes as she let out quiet moans of pleasure. After he licked and sucked every toe, he slowly worked his way up and slowly licked her clit. At that time, Sasha moaned loud with the sound of satisfaction.

This was the first time something like this had ever been done to Sasha and she loved the feeling. Nick licked Sasha into an orgasm within ten minutes, as she released herself on his tongue, he worked his way up to suck on her breast. After that, Nick entered her real slow as she began to scream while he gave her very slow strokes. She wrapped her legs around him and hugged him the whole time. Nick couldn't hold back from releasing his sperm inside of her after no longer than five minutes. He moaned as he let it off in her. He was weak down to his knees, so he just laid on top of Sasha. He laid there for no longer than five minutes before Sasha said she wanted some more. This time he turned her around and put her on all fours. He gently licked her butthole and vagina from behind, until she couldn't hold herself up anymore. That's when he entered her from behind and gave her slow but hard pumps, as her large firm ass bounced Nick back to his starting position every time he pumped. Sasha moaned with pleasure until Nick came again inside of her. She couldn't believe how good Nick was making her feel and he couldn't believe how good she felt. They were under water cruising the ocean having the most romantic time ever, watching sharks, dolphins, and other fish swim by. Nick thought to himself that he had the world in his hands, as Dru Hill played from the surround system speakers.

Sasha sat there when they finished making love thinking about how she held on to her promise of not having sex until she was married. All of Sasha's friends were sexually active and for the first time, now she could see what all the hype was about. She was cruising the bottom of the ocean with her one and only husband. She looked around at all the luxury and for the first time she could see how much effort Nick had put into making this honeymoon special for her. There was a painting of one of her and Nick's first pictures hanging from the top of the submarine that she hadn't even noticed at first. After noticing it, she turned around and thanked Nick while climbing on top of him for more sex at the same time.

The time they spent with each other only made them even closer to one another. They talked about each other's likes, dislikes, dreams, and everything else on each other's minds. They made love several times.

Nick wanted oral sex but didn't pressure Sasha because

he knew she was a rookie to the head game. They used

the whole seven days in the submarine to learn more

and more about one another, also they ate good food

and relaxed. When they left the submarine, they both

wanted to go back under water, but instead they

boarded a cruise ship and headed over to Cancun.

While in Cancun, they stayed in a five-star hotel and

enjoyed every great feature Cancun had to offer. Nick

left Sasha in the room by herself a few times to go

make runs, but he always returned with gifts for her.

Sasha couldn't believe she was so happy. Her every

thought was about Nick.

 Sasha thought about the effort Nick put into

trying to get her attention. She knew if he hadn't of

seen her and Drea for lunch that day, she would have

never called him. Now as she laid in the bed in Cancun,

she was happy he did come back around. Sasha's life

was just starting and for that she was very grateful.

Nick was teaching her as they went, but she still knew a lot about how to keep her husband happy from watching her mom and dad for so many years. From that point forward, Sasha knew her life would never be the same as it used to be, her duty was now to keep her husband happy.

Nick made many mistakes before in the past, so he knew what not to do in order to keep a woman. He knew he had an innocent wife this time around. After all, he had just broken through her unbroken tissue and took her virginity. He knew he had weird sexual interests, a temper at times, and a passion for expensive things, but he knew he would never let anything get in the way of his love for Sasha. It was a lot Nick would have to tame, but for love he knew he would do whatever it was he had to do to.

CHAPTER 5

After returning to Indianapolis, Sasha got her belongings from her mother's house and moved them to her and Nick's six-bedroom house in an expensive suburb of Indianapolis called Geist. Along with six bedrooms the house had a sunroom, playroom, an in-house swimming pool, and sat on a reservoir with a boat and jet skis docked. Nick even had an eight-car garage on the house, with the rest of his cars being parked at his warehouse storage. The house was just amazing, and you would never have to worry about television with the in-house movie theater. Sasha mentioned to Nick that she wanted to keep her job because she didn't want to feel like a leech living so lavage without working her own job. Nick told her that she was his wife and that made her half owner of everything he had including his multi-million-dollar enterprise just as he told her before. She just went with it.

Upon Sasha coming in to take her place in the enterprise she gave Rebecca and Nathan better positions than they ever imagined. Over a short period of time the three had booked over forty new contracts with the city of Indianapolis, for construction and trash dumping. They bought more than thirteen new foreclosed homes that really needed no repairs at all. Nick was very surprised, satisfied and pleased with the progress they had made for the enterprise in such a short time. He purchased more equipment to take on the new contracts plus gave Rebecca and Nathan a nice bonus, along with giving other members bonuses as well.

After a long day at work, Sasha and Nick headed to their palace in Geist. They stopped off at Mr. Dan's on the east side of Indianapolis to order food because neither felt like cooking dinner. Once they arrived home Nick mentioned to Sasha that oral sex was important to him. She told him that she had never done it before, and it grossed her stomach to even think about it. Sasha went on to explain to Nick that she didn't even know what to do anyway. That's when Nick told her she could watch porn to figure it out.

"If you're my wife Sasha, you're supposed to please me in bed. That's what keeps men from cheating," said Nick as he tried to reason with Sasha.

"I want to please you in every way Nick, you are my king, but you have to understand that I've never done that before. I'll have to get prepared for it," replied Sasha. Sasha had a very sad look on her face while saying this. After only being married for a little over three months this was not the way she wanted to feel.

"Well, I'm a do what I have to do then bitch, fuck it," said Nick in a loud tone!

"Why are you talking to me like this Nick," asked Sasha?

Sasha was seeing another side of Nick that she never even knew existed, she did not want to see this side of Nick. After all he had never even cussed in front of her before. Nick had never raised his voice to Sasha, but during this conversation he did. Sasha sat there listening to Nick looking like a puppet while he stood over her and gave demands. She sat there for a minute and then agreed to watch a porn video with him and perform oral sex like the ladies in the videos. While watching the video, she cried the whole time. Nick seemed to be used to porn because all he did was play with himself while watching the sex scenes of Pinkish, a known porn star.

After watching multiple porn videos, it was time for Sasha to make her husband happy. Nick quizzed her after the movies, I guess to see if she was paying attention or not. Sasha was thinking to herself, what did she get herself into. She also thought to herself that this oral sex stuff must had been very important to Nick, though she didn't know what made it so important. Still fresh to their marriage and she was already being yelled at and told to do things she never imagined doing. Nick had pleased himself with his hand a couple times in front of Sasha while watching the videos. Then he asked her if she was ready, she dreadfully said yes.

"Bitch, you're not doing it like Pinkish. I give you the world and you can't even suck my dick right. I'm a get on Back Page and get me a bitch over her to suck my dick while you watch, maybe then you'll get it right since it's in person," said Nick as he stopped her from performing oral sex on him.

Sasha jumped to her feet and ran to the bathroom, after locking herself in she started crying instantly. Nick went into his phone to find a prostitute from Back Page. This situation really had Nick seriously mad. He knew he would have to divorce her if she couldn't get her head game right. He connected with a lady off Back Page and was ready for action. At that time, he wasn't worried about hurting Sasha's feelings or nothing, he just wanted oral sex and how he wanted it to be performed was the sloppy way.

"Just be ready to watch once she gets here, so you'll learn and I won't have to call another bitch again," said Nick to Sasha as he stood outside the bathroom door.

A little while later the doorbell rang. A beautiful Latino came walking in the house. Nick persuaded Sasha to come out of the bathroom and watch him receive oral sex, in the bed that only him and Sasha was supposed to occupy. The woman took her clothes off and gave Nick oral sex. Nick moaned and groaned the whole time before releasing himself all in the woman's face and mouth. Sasha sat there and looked feeling disgusted and humiliated. Nick then told Sasha to come and suck his dick until it was back hard again while being coached by the prostitute. Sasha refused and ran out of the room. Nick paid the prostitute four-hundred dollars and sent her on her way after telling her he would be calling her back for sure.

After the prostitute left, Nick found Sasha in the house and began to sweet talk her and tell her he loved her. He also explained to her that he had to have his pleasure when it came to sex. Sasha then told Nick that she wished he had of mentioned that to her before marriage. For some reason, Nick became irate and smacked Sasha to the floor when she told him that. Sasha then sat there on the floor crying in a cradle position. She had never been abused a day in her life, so it took her by surprise. Nick then told her that she needed to learn how to please a man. He also told her that he was the boss of her, and that it would be in her best interest to never talk to anyone about their personal matters, especially Drea.

Sasha tried to get up and leave the house, but Nick stopped her every time. She couldn't believe what he was taking her through, it was unreal to her. Then to see another woman pleasing him sexually really made her lose her mind. Somehow Nick sweet talked her into thinking that everything he had just done was okay. In Sasha's mind, she knew it was wrong, but the way he persuaded her to think it was okay made her think that maybe she was wrong. He came with bible scriptures and everything to prove he was right, though Sasha never heard it explained the way he did, she just went with it because she felt he did make a valid point.

Over the next several weeks Sasha wasn't the same woman anymore. Everyone could see a change in her but didn't know where the change was coming from. It was like Sasha didn't have the motivation she used to have. Rebecca knew something was wrong with her friend but couldn't get the truth out of her. Nick physically and mentally abused Sasha on different occasions after their initial altercation. On some nights Nick would have other women sleep in the master bedroom with him having sex, while Sasha slept in the guest room hearing moaning all night. All Sasha could do during those times was cry and ask the Lord why. Sasha knew she was being treated unfairly and felt she didn't deserve the treatment. It was like Nick changed into a demon overnight.

Sasha wanted to talk to her loved ones about the situation but was too embarrassed to tell them what was going on. Plus, Nick did make her fearful, so she didn't want to spread their business after he told her not to. All the vehicles Nick had bought for Sasha as wedding gifts were under his control. He went out and bought her a raggedy Chevy Lumina to drive and said she could only drive her new vehicles when they were together. Sasha was upset that she let Nick persuade her to get rid of her beat up Regal. Nick treated her like she was a child on punishment. He let it be known that he had bought everything himself in his house so he would run it the way he wanted to.

Sasha figured she would lie to everyone and tell them she was driving the Lumina because she didn't want to put unnecessary miles on her new vehicles. She knew the first thing Drea would ask after seeing her in the Lumina is where her other cars were at. Though Sasha never cared about what she drove, she still didn't like what was going on. She felt Nick had got her hopes up all for nothing and now she had to lie to everyone in order to cover up everything she was going through. Sasha had never been in a situation in life where she even felt like she needed to lie and now she had to lie to save herself humiliation.

Sasha was just an innocent woman who had never did anyone wrong in her life. Now she was living like she was in prison, getting physically and mentally abused for nothing. Nick did what he wanted to do. He took many trips on his own without Sasha even knowing where he was at. During those times, Nick told her she couldn't have company nor leave the house unless it was for work. She told him she wanted to go to the gym, and he told her to just use the workout equipment at the house. She said to herself that she made the wrong decision by giving up her whole career for Nick. Nick knew Sasha was still young in the mind and wouldn't know what to do so he kept doing what he wanted to do.

Sasha's mom wondered about her daughter. She didn't know what was going on but knew there was something wrong. Nick still acted like he did in the beginning around everyone else, but when alone with

Sasha he was a menace. Sasha didn't know how he could change up the way he had, but just put up with the abuse thinking it would get better over time like Nick promised her. The thing is that Tammy knew her daughter and would figure out what was going on before long. Tammy went to talk to Rebecca and Nathan about this concern and seen that they felt the same way. They all agreed that maybe Sasha was just stressing about her father passing away, which she did do a lot. They knew in time they would know what was going on in Sasha's mind. Not one of them thought it had anything to do with Nick. They just knew for sure Sasha was acting a way they had never seen her act. It didn't have to do with her attitude alone, it was her overall actions and quietness.

Sasha was now totally confused with the concept of marriage. She seen her mother and father happy for many years in their marriage. She knew things like this didn't go on in their marriage and wondered why it was happening with her marriage.

Sasha wanted to know why her mother always preached to her about being a loyal wife to her husband, she wondered if those same morals existed when you were being treated like the animal she was treated as. In the end, all she could do was hope things would go back to the way they were when she first met Nick. Nick seemed to like everyone he hung around in their faces, but behind closed doors he talked bad about all of them, which confused Sasha. Also, behind closed doors, Nick was a true alcoholic who most of the time cried himself to sleep at night.

In time Sasha found out she was pregnant. Once she broke the news to Nick, he was very excited. He started making plans for the baby no sooner than she told him. This truly made Sasha think Nick would change from his evil ways. Their marriage was still fresh, and a baby shouldn't have been the only reason Nick changed, but Sasha wanted the old Nick back and didn't care what it took to make him change as long as he changed. Nick started to loosen up on Sasha and made sure he treated her right. He also made sure he sent her to the best doctor and hospital in Indianapolis for checkups and everything else. He told Sasha to start thinking of names for girls and boys, which they discussed together as an activity. Nick started catering to her every need, he was back to the Nick he used to be and that made Sasha a happy woman.

Sasha told the news of the baby to all her close friends and they were all happy for her. Rebecca was now happy she would have a God daughter or son. Sasha's mom was in total shock and was more than happy to start preparing a room for when her grandchild was to arrive. Sasha knew her mother would be happy for her, she always told Sasha that a child was a blessing. The only problem Sasha knew her mother would have was giving her child back to her, knowing how much her mother loved children. So, in a way Sasha knew there would be no problem finding a babysitter. Her mother told her right away that her child would never have to step foot in a daycare, which was a good thing in Sasha's eyes.

No sooner than two months after finding out about Sasha's pregnancy, Nick started acting up again. First, he was like a dream come true again, but he soon changed back to his old ways. He started back having women coming over to the house sleeping in the room with him, while Sasha either slept in the guest room or in the living room. He made Sasha do all the yard work while pregnant. Sometimes Sasha felt like he made messes in the house just so she would have to clean it up. She told him one day that she was having cramps so she couldn't cook dinner and that's when he picked her small body up by the neck and carried her to the kitchen. He made her cook dinner that night and not just for him, but for the two women he had coming over that night as well. Sasha cried herself to sleep every night. Nick even went as far as to force Sasha to start eating pork which she had never ate in her life. He put a gun to her head at the kitchen table one night until she ate the porkchop he made her fry for herself. It was like she couldn't be herself in any way anymore.

Sasha was sitting at her desk at work talking to a possible new customer for their enterprise as she always did. The possible customer was a man who had a lot of hauling for them to do for his construction company. Seemed that when men came in to talk business, Sasha was always the one to get them to accept the contracts. She never flirted or anything, that's just the way it went. On this day, Nick happened to walk into her office which he never did while she had a client. Nick immediately told the man to get the hell out of his wife's office. Sasha stood up and Nick pushed her back down and grabbed her by the neck. Sasha lost her breath because of how hard he grabbed her neck. He then told her to never smile in another man's face again. Sasha cried and locked herself in her office for hours. She wouldn't even answer when Rebecca came to her office and tried to enter it. Everyone was worried about her. Nick eventually went back in there and demanded her to get herself together or told her there would be problems.

Nick told everyone at work to go home, knowing that Sasha wouldn't come out of her office. He didn't want to break his cover of being such a good man, so sending them home was the only option he had. After all the workers left Nick went into her office and called her soft and told her she just wasn't cut from the same cloth as him. Anything Nick could do to make Sasha feel like it was her fault for his mistreatment, is what he did. Nick was a different man from what others thought and that was the bottom line. He knew the bible and knew how to manipulate the bible to his advantage and make certain verses back up his behavior.

After getting back home from work that day, Nick drastically abused Sasha. He accused her of cheating and flirting. Nick was a jealous guy for no reason. He told her that he would kill her if he ever caught her cheating and her body would never be found. This scared Sasha to the core. She never thought about violence and would have never thought that violence would come to her. In a way, she now felt like she was trapped with Nick. She didn't feel like his wife anymore, she felt more like his child. Nick changed on her in a very short time. She told him that he wasn't the Nick she married, he smacked her and told her to live with it. He was tearing her self-esteem down slowly, but surely, even more than it was already down. Little did he know is that her self-esteem was already down from her ex-boyfriend Ronald cheating on her. Ronald cheated on her and she left him, now Nick was cheating in her face and she felt she had to take it because he was her husband.

No matter what Sasha tried to do to cover up her unhappiness, her close people knew something was going on with her. Sasha stopped attending church like she used to, which she had been every Saturday since she was born. Part of the reason of her not attending church is because Nick really didn't like her going anywhere without him. He didn't like her going anywhere because he knew she always got attention from other men. Though he was sought after by many women, he was still an insecure man on the inside. Sasha just dealt with it and stuck to her death do us part vow.

When the incident in Sasha's office occurred, many other workers heard Nick holler at her. It caught many people by surprise. Though no one said anything to them personally, they did talk amongst each other. The word got back to Rebecca and she was astounded by the news. She knew something wasn't right and she was now seeing what it was. She sat and talked with Sasha, but never brought it up, she just tried to pick Sasha's brain to see if she would bring it up on her own. Rebecca went to Sasha's mother and told her something wasn't right with Sasha and this time Tammy told her they needed to figure out the problem. After they agreed something was wrong, they both called Sasha and told her they wanted to have a talk with her.

Sasha was able to get away from Nick and go to her mom's house. They asked her many questions and one was why she never drove the cars Nick had bought her. They wondered why she drove a raggedy Lumina but had brand-new cars at home. Rebecca mentioned that she heard he had hollered at her at work. They brought up so many issues that all Sasha could do was cry and tell them that Nick had changed on her. She spilled her heart out to them, but she didn't mention that he physically abused her, and cheated on her in their house right in her face. She just told them he was too controlling. Sasha's mom told her many men with money be that way and that's why she should have never quit her job because of him telling her to do so. She told her the game from an older woman's perspective. She also told her not to feel like she had to put up with all his nonsense just because she was married to him and let Sasha know that marriage is a fifty/fifty thing.

Sasha soaked in everything her mother told her. After that Sasha sat around with her mother and Rebecca for as long as she could. She knew Nick would be mad if she came home too late, so she cut her visit short. During the time of the visit, she did get some wisdom from her mother though. She had memories of being in the house with her mother and Rebecca, back when she was truly happy in life. What no one knew, but her is that she didn't want to leave her mother's house from that visit. Being around Nick made her feel some type of way that she just didn't like. She was ready to leave everything and go back home to her mother.

Upon arriving back home, Sasha was surprised by even more disrespect from Nick. He had another woman at their house cooking dinner for him with just an apron and heels on. The woman's thick chocolate ass faced Sasha as the woman cooked on the stove. The woman was thick and beautiful. Sasha was so surprised that before she knew it, she was attacking Nick and crying at the same time. Nick told the woman to continue what she was doing then grabbed Sasha by the neck and carried her to another room.

"Bitch, don't you ever put your hands on me," said Nick as he smacked and shoved his pregnant wife to the couch.

Sasha sat there like an obedient child listening to her husband tell her everything she did wrong. Nick then tried talking Sasha into having a threesome, but she didn't agree with it. When she didn't agree with having a threesome Nick lashed out in even more rage. Telling her that it was either she would have a threesome or they could get a divorce. This caught Sasha by surprise, but she still wouldn't let up, she told him that it would just have to be a divorce. That's when he grabbed her up again and took her upstairs to beat her more. After that he came back downstairs and had sex with the other woman on the kitchen table. Sasha could hear the moaning and groaning all the way upstairs, as she always did. Sasha said to herself that she was done with Nick after this episode.

Nick only went into rage after Sasha said no to the threesome because he thought he had her all the way under control. Men like Nick go through life getting a kick out of other people fearing them. Sasha knew he was a control freak, but she just didn't know he wanted to control her every move. Nick wanted whatever made him happy to make her happy so she would always do what he wanted. Nick didn't want a woman with her own brain, he wanted a woman who would think how he wanted her to think. He didn't want to be the way he was with Sasha, but he thought since she was so young, she would have immediately fell in line. Once Nick seen Sasha didn't fall in line, he felt he needed to make her fear him, so she would fall in line. That was the way he thought.

CHAPTER 6

Drea went to Sasha's workplace to talk to her. She wouldn't take no for an answer when Sasha tried to deny her offer to lunch. Nick wasn't in the office on this day, due to him having to take a trip out of town. Which was a good thing, but he still had his ways of watching Sasha. Drea treated Sasha to lunch at a restaurant called Ocean Prime. Once they sat at the table, Drea told Sasha some very disturbing news. She told her that she knew who Nick was and that he wasn't who he said he was. He was a very wealthy drug lord who only used his businesses to wash his dirty money. Nick's real name was Jamal Jordan and he was a fugitive. Nick had one of Drea's cousin killed years before and that's why Drea remembered his face. Drea remembered seeing Nick on trial, but it was so long before the day she saw him that his face just didn't bring up that memory. Nick beat the case in trial, but everyone knew he put the hit that was behind Drea's cousin getting killed. Drea warned Sasha that Nick was a very dangerous man who was not to be played with.

After hearing what Drea had to say, Sasha got teary eyed and spilled her heart out to Drea. Unlike she did when talking to her mom and Rebecca, she told Drea everything that was going on. Drea was lost for words and cried with her dear friend. Drea then showed Sasha a fully loaded handgun and told her that she would kill Nick and wanted to kill him. Drea then told Sasha all she had to do was say the word and she would kill Nick on site to stop a headache in the future. Drea got so mad that Sasha had to dry her tears and calm Drea down. After Drea calmed down, she told Sasha that she needed to move far away from Nick if she knew what was good for her and her unborn child.

Come to find out Nick was not only the biggest drug dealer in Indianapolis, but he was also dealing big all over the United States. He got his drugs straight from Mexico, which is why he left Sasha in the room by herself so many times on their honeymoon in

Cancun. He had a team of killers that moved at his call anytime and were on a full-time payroll with him. Nick was the big man on the block and got respect wherever he went. No one in the United States had a direct connect with Mexico like Nick did. After finding this out Sasha knew she had to be very careful and that she needed to get away from him immediately.

Drea warned Sasha to never mention anything about their conversation to Nick. Sasha was already on edge with him, but now she had a plan to find out as much information about Nick as she could. Since she was always in the house alone, she figured that wouldn't be a problem, though she knew he did have cameras in the house. With Sasha now just weeks away from having her baby she knew she had to put a plan together fast. She knew she couldn't do anything obvious, but she did know she had to leave Nick soon.

Sasha got back to work and immediately started googling Nick. The name Nick Burton was no good, so she googled his real name, which was Jamal Jordan. To her surprise, a whole story came across the screen about him. She found out he was a fugitive who was wanted in eight different states. He had seventeen children, but only told her about one. He had another wife under his real name, plus they said they didn't know how many more he had. He had houses in practically every state, with women occupying each one while he was gone. He had done over fifteen years in prison for murder. And to say the least he was nothing to be played with. They labeled him a master mind criminal. He had many different law enforcement officials on his payroll and could find out anything about anybody. The police knew Nick had corrupt cops on his payroll and warned everyone to stay away from him and to call the FBI, not the local police immediately if they were to see him.

After coming home Sasha felt very uneasy. Nick came in from his trip being nice to her for some reason. He cooked dinner for the two of them and ordered new movies from Netflix for them to watch. He explained to her that he loved her more than life and apologized for the way he had been treating her. He told her that his childhood wasn't the best and he carried the resentment in his heart, but she was bringing the hurt out of him because she was showing him real love. He massaged her whole body and made love to her passionately. Then he told her he would be going out of town the next morning on a business trip and she could go with him if she wanted, which she told him she would stay home.

Sasha met up with Drea everyday Nick was gone, getting help on a plan to leave him. She said she didn't want to snitch on him, but she did want to be done with him. Drea told her to just hang in there until she could leave peacefully and have everything she needed. Now that Nick was in control of everything it would be hard for her to leave with money. Drea hooked Sasha up with a gun and told her to keep it somewhere close, but still hidden. Drea couldn't help, but to feel sorry for Sasha because she knew she was a good person. Though she was in a tricky situation, Drea knew things would work out for the best because God was on their side.

At this time Drea was the only one Sasha could count on to keep things a secret. After all it was Drea who told her to watch him in the first place. Sasha told Drea about all the information she had found out about Nick and Drea told her to not be afraid of him. She assured Sasha that she would kill him herself if he caused her anymore harm. Drea also told her to come back to Nordstrom and get her job back. Sasha told her she would do so after everything was taken care of with Nick. Sasha really wondered how she could be in this situation and she did nothing wrong. She also thought about the fact that she was married to a man who wasn't even married under his real name. In all actuality, she didn't know the man she gave her virginity up to and was having her first baby with.

Nick returned from out of town still in a good mood. He talked to Sasha more about what to name the baby. Since they were having a boy Sasha told him that he could name him. She was caught by surprise when he told her he wanted to name him Jamal. She acted like she didn't know what was going on and agreed to name their son Jamal. It was a good sign to her that he did want his son to have his real name. At the same time, she knew he wasn't to be trusted and she needed to leave him as soon as possible. Nick told her about a trip he booked for them to go to the Virgin Islands. He told her he wanted to take the baby with them as well. She didn't like the sound of it, but still agreed to it anyway.

As Nick and Sasha sat there talking, he had to walk away to answer his phone. When he came back into the room his whole attitude was different. He asked her why she never told him she went to lunch with Drea while he was gone on his last trip. He also told her to stay away from Drea or he would make sure she stayed away from her himself. Sasha told him that Drea was her friend and she had the right to be around her and that's when he smacked her so hard that she passed out.

He blacked her eye and busted her lip with just one smack. When she woke up, she headed straight for the door. She ran out the house crying and saying, "help me." To her dissatisfaction, no one heard her, no cars were riding down the street and no neighbors seemed to see what was going on in the wee hours of the night. Nick chased her down and brought her back to their house. He then tied her up to a chair and tried to apologize and tell her that she caused him to smack her. In a way, he was trying to hypnotize her into believing it was all her fault. He told her that she couldn't leave the house until her face was healed, which she agreed to him otherwise she knew he wouldn't have untied her.

Sasha sat in the house for weeks before she healed up. Nick was there to cater to her every need. He even cried to her at times. She was really feeling sorry for him, so she quit her little investigations and said she would stand by her husband. She started avoiding Drea's calls and everything. Sasha said in her mind that from that day forward she would give her husband her all and do everything to make him happy. He even talked her into letting another woman eat her pussy. Though Sasha didn't want to and on top of that she was pregnant, she still had let the woman eat her out. She felt violated afterwards, but still liked the fact that she pleased her husband. Nick was very pleased, as he sat recording the sexual encounter he smiled and told Sasha he loved her the whole time. When Sasha seen him recording the scene, she knew it would come back to haunt her, but she just went with it anyway.

Nick woke up in the middle of the night having to rush out the house fast. Sasha just let him go without asking questions. A little while later, Nick pulled up to Hawthorne projects with his pistol in hand. It was obvious he was mad about the phone call he received while in bed at three in the morning. He got a call that one of his workers was snorting his product and tricking off his money on women. To make up for the losses the worker would make bags shorter for the customers. Nick went in the apartment dressed in an all-black Polo sweat suit with the black Timberlands to match. Lil Dre never seen it coming, but Nick stepped straight to him and blew his brains out without even a blink. Then Nick looked at everyone else in the room, that's when everyone in the room bowed their heads. Nick then told them the new way things would be and jumped back in his black Corvette and hit the gas before the police came.

Only a few people knew the story behind Nick. He was black, but still was a member of the Mexican cartel. His ruthlessness and love for money got him his position. He committed his first murder when he was only eight years old and had done many more since then. He was not to be played with and could laugh with you knowing he had a hit man coming to kill you any second. He moved under over twenty different aliases. He had sacrificed a lot in life to show his loyalty to the Mexican cartel. He even sacrificed his ex-wife's life to show the cartel he would put them before anyone. They told him to kill her himself after she ran off with money and that's what he did. That's the reason why his daughter moved away from him and never turned back, she knew he was the reason her mother was dead but didn't know he was the one who pulled the trigger. If his daughter had of known, he pulled the trigger it would have only made the situation worst.

Nick pulled back up to his house seeing ambulances all around. He ran into the house and found them taking Sasha out to have the baby. He shed tears of joy when he seen what was going on. He hurried upstairs to change clothes. Then he jumped in his money green Hummer H1 on thirty-six-inch rims to follow the ambulance to Carmel Saint Vincent hospital. He bumped Mr. Bigg "take that shit to trial" and shook his head grooving the whole way there. He called everyone to tell them the baby was about to be born. He was like a child on Christmas day opening gifts, all about his baby boy.

While at the hospital, Nick paced back and forth waiting for his baby boy to take his first breath on earth. Sasha's mom, Rebecca and Nathan came to the hospital to be with Nick, Sasha and the baby. Sasha had finally called Drea, but Drea was a no show at the time. Nick had bought the baby so much stuff that the baby wouldn't be able to use all of it even if he were to be born three times. You would have thought this was Nick's first child, but many didn't know he had seventeen other children. Nick was truly a character.

Sasha's mom asked Nick about his family and why they weren't at the hospital and why he never talked about them. He made up excuses that they just didn't talk to him because they were jealous of his success. What she didn't know is that his family cut him off because he was responsible for the deaths of his little brother, uncle and father. Nick used to send them to California and Texas to pick up packages for him. When he sent them on their last and final trip for him, he never told them that the Mexicans wanted to kill him. Since they couldn't get him, they got his runners instead and Nick wouldn't even pay for their funerals. He acted like it was their fault they were dead and not his. After this incident, the whole family cut Nick off and he really didn't care because he still had his money.

Meanwhile, Drea was collecting all the information she could about Nick. She went around to all her family members in every hood she knew in Indianapolis asking questions. It was like Nick was a different person to everyone she talked to. Some said he was the nicest man on earth, some said he was the meanest. One of her uncles from a neighborhood called Haughville even said him and Nick used to go to church together. He said Nick used to do many charity events for anyone who needed help. He said Nick was married to a beautiful Brazilian woman at that time, but she ended up moving back to Brazil for a reason no one knew, except her and Nick. Drea couldn't believe all the different stories she heard about Nick, it was like no one even knew the true him, but she knew the truth. She didn't care about Sasha not taking her calls she was still going to get to the bottom of everything and even kill him when time permitted it. Drea had low key got her a team together for Nick and it was a team that would surprise him. He killed Lil Dre in Hawthorne and that's where Drea was from. She had enough influence to get them to turn on Nick and she silently did so. After all everyone was after money and power, so getting Nick out the way would only open the streets for the up and coming.

The baby was delivered! He came out with a head full of hair and weighed almost eleven pounds. Nick had a photographer there to take every picture. Nick cried at the first site of his little boy. Nick was a very happy man! Sasha couldn't hold the baby five minutes without Nick trying to take him back, which did make her smile. Nick apologized to everyone about how overprotective he was about his son, but he explained to them that his son was bringing light back to his dark life. They all told him he was fine, and they were happy for him, his son, and Sasha. Nick told the photographer to snap away from every angle of the room. Nick then pulled out the Louis Vuitton carry-on bag full of designer clothes and shoes to dress his son.

Sasha sat in the hospital for three days before she was released to go home. Upon arriving at home, she noticed a different car in the driveway. Nick then told her that he hired a nanny to help her around the house. Sasha smiled because Nick was always so thoughtful. It was like he had an answer for every question, even the questions that weren't even asked. The nanny greeted them at the door. She was a short thick chocolate woman, and she was a very beautiful woman. Sasha just knew Nick wouldn't try to get them all to sleep together, but she was preparing for it if he did. She was willing to do whatever to be a family with her child and Nick. Sasha let that thought pass through her mind and went to get everything situated in her son's room.

Sasha looked at her phone and seen multiple missed text messages from Drea. She looked at them and then erased them. She wasn't going to do anything against her husband. Sasha felt he deserved another chance and that's what she was going to give him. She made a promise to herself that she would never put anyone in their business again. She made a mental note that she would get back with Drea, but not any time soon. She felt she needed to build more with her husband and son first and that's what her mind was determined to do.

Sasha couldn't have sex for a few weeks after she gave birth, but as soon as the time period was over with, Nick was ready. Sasha got off work, picked up her son from her mothers, and headed home. No sooner than she walked in the door she seen Nick had the nanny bent over on the back of the couch stroking her. He told her to put the baby down and come join. This really shocked her because she had her son in her arms. She told him no. That's when he went back to his old ways and chased her down demanding her to come join. She still refused and he started choking her. He choked her so much that even the nanny came to try and get him off her. He turned around and smacked the nanny to the ground too. The nanny tried to leave, but he grabbed her and told her he would kill her if she stepped out the door. He then told the nanny that he pays her to do what he tells her, really telling her to fall in line with what he says and agree with what he does.

The nanny just took what Nick threw out there, she really needed the job. When she first took the job, Nick told her sex would be involved, but since she knew he had a wife she thought him, and Sasha were swingers and Sasha would join them. After seeing how Nick was doing things the nanny was now very uncomfortable. The nanny was good looking herself, thick and a freak. She previously was in the porn industry but changed her life and got into doing live in assistance. In no way did she plan on having to disrespect a woman of a house though. She was a woman who wouldn't just stand for anything to receive money, even though she had sold her body before.

When the day turned to night, Nick told Sasha that she was on punishment and had to sleep in the guest room. He took their son and the nanny and slept in the master bedroom. Sasha cried herself to sleep that night. He had the nanny in her room taking care of her son like she was his mother. This situation really hurt Sasha to the core. The nanny told Sasha on the low the next day that she only did it because Nick made her do so. In which Sasha did understand, but it still didn't take away the pain she felt. At this point, Sasha made up her mind that she had to leave Nick and that was final. Nick took her phone so she couldn't call anyone, but she knew she would leave him the first chance she got. She didn't care about the threats anymore, she refused to have her son around that type of behavior.

Sasha thought about the way Nick just abused her in front of her son. She thought about how much Nick had hidden from her. The fact that he wanted her to watch him have sex with other women and most of the time join him, demanding threesomes. Lastly, she thought about all the physical abuse Nick was putting her through. Sasha knew she couldn't take anymore. Her mother raised her to submit to her husband but didn't raise her to be a fool for her husband.

The next day after getting her phone, Sasha immediately called Drea. They had small talk about what happened the night before to Sasha and Drea recommended a book for Sasha to read, that was wrote by a guy from her neighborhood who was a thug gone legit. The book was called Women Stop Falling 4 No Good Men. Drea said she wanted her to start reading the book and then talk to her. Drea did it this way because she wanted Sasha to see what a woman shouldn't be treated like and for Sasha to see what another man had to say about no good men and their characteristics. So, Sasha agreed to read the book and went to Amazon to order the Kindle version on her phone. Drea told her to learn some things about herself as she knew the book would awaken Sasha to the many

strengths she already possessed.

CHAPTER 7

Sasha had been away from Nick for over a month and he still pestered her. She left with nothing at all. Not that Nick would have given her anything anyway. She waited until he was gone one day, packed her son's belongings and headed out. She had Drea pick her up, leaving the cars and everything. The nanny left at the same time and told Sasha how sorry she was about what she was going through. Nick was highly upset when he came home to an empty house. He immediately started to call Sasha's phone. She wouldn't answer at first, then he threatened to put the video out of their threesome, so she gave in.

He promised her many things if she was to come back, but she told him she couldn't do it. Now that her mother, Rebecca and Nathan knew the way he treated her, they influenced her in every way they could to stay away from him. Plus, she was into the book that Drea told her to read and seen the way Nick treated her all through the book. Sasha knew she deserved better and she wouldn't settle for less anymore. She wasn't only living for her anymore, but also for her son. The author of the book Eric Williams had all his contact information in the book and Sasha used it to ask him many questions. After talking to Eric, Sasha agreed to listen to his lectures online and to start attending his battered women groups.

Nick popped up at Sasha's mother house on his own free will. Sasha's mother told him to get away from her door and to never step foot on her property again. She threatened to call the police on him and that's when he got mad. He kicked in the door, went in and started to choke Sasha and her mother. He then tried to grab his son and run for the door but tripped and fell after Sasha put her leg out to trip him. By that time people in the neighborhood started to gather around and the police were on the way. Nick then ran to his candy red Aston Martin and hit the road. Before leaving he looked back at Sasha and told her to remember he would kill her if she told the police who he was.

Sasha's mother told her to tell anyway, but after Sasha told her a little more about Nick she quickly agreed not to tell too.

Rebecca had quit working for Nick's enterprise, but Nathan decided to stay. Nick was no different towards him and Nathan was no different towards Nick. Part of the reason Nathan was no different is because he didn't know the full story of what happened with Sasha. In his mind, they were just in an argument and would be back together soon. Nick tried his best to keep Nathan on his team since he was the only one left out of the crew who would even talk to him.

Sasha had just got done feeding the baby, then went to turn on the five o'clock news. The top story was a woman murdered and multiple shootings in the Indianapolis area. Headline story was of a woman shot while leaving Lafayette Square Mall. They said someone must have sat and waited on her to exit the mall and upon her arrival to her car she was shot twice in the head. Then when the picture of the woman came up, Sasha started to cry because it was the nanny who Nick had hired to work for them. Sasha ran to her mom crying and telling her she thought Nick was behind the murder because the woman knew too much information. Sasha couldn't watch any more. She took her an extra dose of sleeping pills and went to sleep.

Sasha remembered all the information the nanny had given her, so she called the nannies family to tell them what she felt. To Sasha's surprise the family didn't even seem to care about the young woman being murdered. Then when Sasha told them Nick's name, they told her to not call their home again. Sasha hung up the phone surprised that someone would be that way with their own flesh and blood. No matter what Sasha knew she would seek justice for the young lady because she was murdered for nothing and Nick had to be stopped.

The time was two thirty a.m. when Sasha was awakened by her phone ringing. It was Drea telling her that she needed to talk to her in person immediately.

Sasha told her to come to her mom's house to talk. When Drea got there, she told her that Nick had been shooting at her and was in her job everyday talking to her coworker Tonya, who never liked Sasha when she worked there. She told her that Nick was showering Tonya with gifts just like he was doing her in the beginning. Drea said every chance Nick got, he was over there threatening her too. She said he told her that he knew she was the one who helped Sasha get away from the house and he would get her for it. Then the day before when she was on her way home from work someone pulled up on her at the stop light and started to shoot at her. Luckily Drea was no stranger to danger and immediately retrieved her weapon to fire back, and that's when the car sped off. To Drea's surprise she did shoot and kill one of the occupants in the car from what she seen on the news. It was a guy from her neighborhood who worked for Nick, that's what let her know Nick was behind the attempted ambush.

Drea was questioned by the police after the shooting occurred. She was very calm about the whole situation. She told them she was just trying to defend herself by shooting back to keep whoever it was from shooting her. After Drea and witnesses told police that the car pulled up on Drea and opened fire, they considered it self-defense. They still took Drea's gun but did tell her she would get it back. Drea couldn't believe she had just murdered someone and to think of how quick it happened made her say, "wow."

The city of Indianapolis was now in an uproar. The city was known for having its spurts of violence and everyone suspected drugs, but this was something totally different. The good thing going for Sasha is that she had Drea on her side and Drea wasn't a stranger to danger. They sat there and came up with a plan for Nick and he wouldn't be happy with the results, or so they thought. Nick had a plan of his own that would shock them all. He had movers move all his stuff out the house and put Nathan in charge of the enterprise while he disappeared to somewhere, they would never figure out.

Over the next couple months no one heard a word from Nick. He was like a ghost to everyone who knew him. Sasha was busy trying to get things in her life back together. Drea tried to get her to go back to Nordstrom, but she refused and started a job as a manager at McDonald's. In no way was this easy for Sasha. With no car, she just rode a bike to work. She wanted to do everything on her own after she learned a valuable lesson from Nick. Men were always trying to pick her up, but she kept on about her business. When it would rain, she would catch the Indygo bus and just put her bike on the front of the bus to ride when she got off. She was suffering, but she stayed with hope so that kept a smile on her face. She may have been working for a little over minimum wage, but she knew it was just a hurdle to jump on her way to living independent.

Sasha thought about how she just gave everything up when Nick told her to give it up. She knew she made a mistake by doing so, but now it was too late to say no and to feel sorry for herself. She just rolled with the punches. She often wondered what happened to her money that was in her savings when she did move with Nick. It seemed he showered her with so much that she lost track of her own money, and it was gone to who knew where. Sasha was laughed at by most women who seen her, they called her stupid for leaving Nick. They laughed at her because she went from a million-dollar home to working at McDonald's, and whenever she was seen at the bus stop, she was clowned by many in Indianapolis traffic. Sasha just took these things in and went about her business.

Nathan was the man running the show at the enterprise. Even without a word from Nick he was keeping things rolling and was doing better without Nick than with him. Rebecca was working a good job for a student loan management company called Sallie Mae, so things were on the right path for them. They were still worried about Sasha and it didn't make it no better that she wouldn't take any help from anyone. They knew somehow things would work out though. They both just wished Sasha would take some help from them. Sasha was looked at like a bum on the streets and Rebecca nor Nathan, liked that about their friend. On the other hand, they knew Sasha didn't care about what no one thought of her, they also knew that Sasha was a determined woman and would come up before long.

Meanwhile, Nick was chilling in his beach house with his wife and kids. The alias he used for this identity was John Terry. He worked as a traveling engineer there in California, also him and his wife together were the owners of multiple businesses and enterprises. He made a good living for himself and no one knew who he really was, not even his wife. Her name was Kim and she came from a wealthy family herself. Though she was Caucasian she had the body of a stallion. She was one to make any man look twice for sure. Nick didn't treat her like he did Sasha because he knew she had too much pull in law enforcement, with her brother being a judge. Nick did use all her pull to his benefit though. He could find out anything about anyone in California. He also had many of the crooked cops working for him. On this day, he had a plan. He called one of the cops on his payroll and asked for a favor. Nick wanted twelve swat uniforms. Though it was a weird command, his worker still got them for him. The next day, Nick was on a flight heading to Mexico.

Drea finally talked Sasha into going to dinner with her. They went to Ruth's Chris on the north side of Indianapolis. They discussed the book, Women Stop Falling 4 No Good Men, and to Sasha's surprise Drea had the author Eric Williams come there to meet her, though Sasha and Eric had already talked on the phone without Drea knowing. This was in no way a hook up, Drea just wanted Sasha to get some advice from him. Eric had helped Drea so much that she knew he could help Sasha as well. The three sat at the table and the first thing Sasha said was she didn't want him to danger himself from being around her. Eric knew about her situation and assured her that all three of them were all right. Eric had his past in the streets and in no way, was he to be played with. What Sasha didn't know is that Eric was a previous robber and used to extort Nick out of thousands of dollars. Eric knew that Nick knew to choose his battles wisely.

They sat at the table and talked about many relationship issues. Sasha had talked to Eric on the phone, but in no way, did she really plan on going to his meetings or meeting him in person even though she said she would. Now she felt she had to commit to his meetings, being that Drea made her meet him face to face. They ate good and even had a few cocktails. Eric had set up for Sasha to come to his facility for a meeting and even offered her housing assistance, but she refused. He told her there was many women he coached that had been through many situations like hers and there was light at the end of the tunnel. Sasha for some reason believed him and said she would go under one condition and that was that he could never put her name on any paperwork. He agreed and it was a done deal after that.

After getting home Sasha's mom was there waiting for her and gave her a hug as soon as she came in the door. It was odd for Sasha, but she knew her mother loved her. Sasha's mother told her that her ex-boyfriend Ronald had called her and told her some disturbing news. He told her that Nick was very dangerous and when Nick had talked to him about not communicating with Sasha anymore, he hung him over the bridge sitting over White River and made him promise not to say a word to Sasha again. Ronald only built up the courage to call at this time because he finally contacted the police, though they couldn't find any information on Nick and it was just hearsay, he was still able to get a no contact order. What was even more disturbing is that Nick also used to date Ronald's mother. He told them that Nick had called a week before and had his mother out in the middle of the night transporting dope for him. Ronald said his mother told him to warn Sasha to do what Nick said or it would be big trouble.

By this time nothing anyone said surprised Sasha anymore, so she took it in one ear, and it went out the other. She knew what type of man Nick was, but she knew she prayed to an awesome God, so she feared nothing. Sasha was now focused on healing and getting things back on track. She wanted to get enrolled in college again and pick up where she left off, of course with the responsibility of her son now. So far so good is what she saw it as. She had her meetings set up with the author now, so she was going to see if his groups would bring any type of closure to her situation.

The next day at work for Drea was drastic. For some reason, Tonya kept staring at her and giving her a mean look. Before you knew it, Drea was following Tonya to the restroom. After entering the restroom Drea started beating Tonya up like she stole something from her. She stomped her and even spit on her, without no one even knowing what was going on. Drea told her that if anything happened to her friend, she would be the first one she came to kill. Tonya knew that Drea's words were for real but thought because she now dealt with Nick nothing could happen to her. Unlike Sasha, Tonya knew the power Nick had out in the streets and loved it.

Sasha went to work with the same attitude she always had. In no way, would anyone know she was going through the hell she was going through. After work her plan was to go to a meeting with the author and other women he coached. On this day, Sasha was offered the position of becoming the district manager of McDonald's. Sasha couldn't help, but to accept the position as it would give her a generous raise and put her well on the way to getting her life back together. With the new position, Sasha, would be running more than one McDonald's and that would keep her busy like she wanted. She figured the busier she stayed, the less she would think about her situation.

Sasha went to the meeting with Eric. She rode her bike to the meeting and was happy she did after she seen how many women were there. Eric stood up and did a speech and for some reason every word he said touched Sasha in an emotional way. Two women came to Sasha and asked her to become a part of their team. What Eric did was break the women up into teams so they would all be each other's support in a small group, instead of everyone just being a big group. He wanted them to have small groups so they could really get to know each other. Sasha teamed up with two ladies named Sarah and Valarie.

Sarah had come from an abusive marriage. Her husband used to also drug her and sell her for sex while she was drugged up. Her husband also filmed the gang rapes, which is how she found out what was going on. She was going through their drawers one day in their bedroom and came up on one of the many tapes recorded by him. She couldn't believe what she discovered. Then on top of that one of the regulars who used to pay her husband to have sex with her fell in love with her. He really didn't know she was drugged and thought she liked the sex by the way she moaned. He ended up at her house one day while her husband was gone and asked her to leave with him, but she refused. After her discovery, she left her husband and threatened to bring the police into the situation if he didn't leave her alone. When Sarah got with Tim, she got with him because his money infatuated her. She didn't know until she found the tape that she eventually became one of his biggest money makers.

Valarie was an older lady, but still looked young. She owned a hair salon and was very successful at what she did. Her problem was meeting younger men who only used her. By this time, she was broke but still making it and in the beginning stages of filing bankruptcy. Her previous boyfriend took her for everything she had plus more. He never beat her physically, but the mental abuse he put her through made her wish he would have just physically beat her instead and left her alone. She had been in Eric's program for a while now and was building herself back up and thanks to her clientele she kept money flowing in and at a constant flow. She was able to keep some customers from her old salon and was trying hard to save and open another one.

The three of them sat in their little circle talking about life in general. Sasha was able to tell Sarah and Valarie her story, but she didn't give full details. Sasha really felt good about herself after releasing the nature of her problems to women who had been through similar things themselves. The women comforted her and let her know they had her back. Valarie told Sasha that the weather was about to break into winter, and she had a car for her free of charge. Sasha first refused of course but gave in and accepted the car after a while. The car was a nice one, a 2004 Buick Lasabre. The car was one thing Valarie kept after getting ripped off by her ex. They all exchanged phone numbers and planned for Sasha to pick up the car the following day. Sasha didn't jump up and start clapping her hands, however she was happy about Valarie giving her a car and was very grateful. She must have told Valarie thank you over a million times. Valarie seen Sasha ride up on a bike and knew off top she was going to give her the car.

Sasha called and thanked Drea immediately after the meeting. She told Drea that she would never miss a meeting and told her about how she felt at home during the meeting because the people were so welcoming. She felt she had known everyone in the meeting for a lifetime. Drea didn't bother to tell Sasha about the incident with Tonya at work, because she wanted Sasha to stay in her positive mind state. So, they just chatted a while and got off the phone.

Sasha was back to her old days of keeping a goals list, keeping written affirmations everywhere she frequently went and praying every night. She looked at her goals list and seen since she didn't have to buy a car anymore, she would get her an apartment instead. With the district manager's position at McDonald's Sasha knew she would be getting an apartment in no time. Sasha felt she was getting back to her normal mind state more and more by the minute. Though she did think about Nick, she in no way wanted him back in her life.

CHAPTER 8

Life had just gotten better for Sasha. She was on the roll like she hit big at the Casino. She had a good paying position at her job, built a firm support group, and on top of that Eric was helping her file for divorce. Nick was still nowhere to be found. Then one day out the clear blue sky he called Sasha. He told her, her everyday schedule, from that moment on she paced back and forth in her room until the time she went to bed. Sasha asked Nick to please just leave her alone. Nick cussed her out and told her to simply do what he said, or it would be consequences. He wanted to see his son, when she told him she couldn't do it his temper struck and he cussed her out even more, then hung up the phone. He had made no effort to see his son in the five months he vanished but was now threatening her to see him.

Three days later, Sasha was at work when her phone started ringing. She normally didn't answer her phone at work, but she answered this time for a strange number. It was ADT security systems calling her to tell her the alarm had sounded in her mother's house. They told her they had called out to the house, but no one answered the phone. That's when Sasha dropped the Mc Double, she was making and rushed home.

Upon getting home, Sasha saw police officers surrounding the house. They asked who she was and once she told them who she was they let her go to open the front door so officers could enter the house. They pushed her to the side immediately after she opened the door and rushed in the house. Sasha's heart dropped when they told her no one was in the house. No trace of her mother or son was in the house. She didn't know what to think. She immediately called Drea, Rebecca and Eric. They all arrived and then Sarah and Valarie pulled up a short time later. Sasha gave the police a police report, but the police told her that she couldn't file her mother or son missing for another seventy-two hours. She could only cry at this time because she knew what had happened, she just prayed Nick had enough love in his heart to not kill her mother and child.

Neighbors told Sasha that eight to ten vans pulled up that looked like undercover police vans. They said all the men had police badges around their necks when they went up to the house. They said they didn't think anything was wrong because all the men had SWAT team uniforms on as well and it didn't look like any foul play. All the neighbors went on about their day, not knowing their neighbor was being kidnapped at the time. After Sasha heard that, she had no choice but to call the police and tell them everything she found out about Nick. They issued out an Amber Alert for her son and a description of Nick, along with the description of her mother. The police said Nick had been on the FBI's most wanted list for years now. They were trying to catch him silently, so they never aired him on TV. They knew with his status he could be anywhere, so they just worked off what they knew in a silent manner. They knew about many of his aliases, but didn't know them all, hoping that someday someone would come forward with the information they needed.

Sasha was another woman after the kidnapping situation happened. She went and retrieved the gun Drea had given her and was determined to go on the mission to find her son and mother. She had her crew with her but told them to stay away so she could handle her business, though no one listened. Eric had his Cadillac Escalade outside, so the crew piled in it and headed to his house. At his house is where they formulated a plan. The good thing working on Sasha's behalf is that she had Eric and Drea working with her, and they really knew the street life. Eric promised her they would find her mother and son. Though he couldn't promise her they would be alive when they found them.

Meanwhile, Sasha's mother was in the back of a van with her grandson. She couldn't see where she was going due to the clothed black bag over her face. She never begged for her life; her only concern was her grandson. The van finally stopped, that's when she heard Nick's voice. He took the bag off her face and asked her how his workers treated her. She told him that she was thrown into the van. Nick then asked her who threw her, then after there was no answer, he pulled out his gun and shot two of his workers in the head. He then grabbed his son and started to hug and kiss him. He explained to Sasha's mother that he didn't want to hurt anyone but wanted to see his son, so he had to do what he had to do to make it happen. He explained that he would let her go, but she had to tell the police she left on her own just needing time away. They were talking as they stepped into a house out of a garage. Sasha's mom was lost for words when she stepped inside. She stepped into a true mansion. As she looked out the patio all she could see was land, so she knew she was somewhere no one could find her at. All she could see was horses, cows and hogs from her view.

As Sasha's mother talked to Nick, which was a serious conversation, the two men who were killed by Nick were being carried around to the back yard where Tammy and Nick both could see the bodies. They were then thrown into the hog pen. The hogs devoured their whole bodies, bones and all. That's when Nick turned to her and told her he was tired of living the way he was. They talked for hours about what bothered him. She gave Nick the best advice she could. Nick broke out into tears on more than one occasion during their conversation. Then when she asked him why he would go to such an extreme to see his son, he told her that it was the only thing he felt he had left to do. She just told him to pray. He asked her to pray with him, then they got down on their knees and prayed, as their arms rested on the plush burgundy couch. He told her that he just wanted to spend a couple days with his son and would let them go, and to make herself at home. She agreed and went to the room he had prepared for her. What was in the room was more than she could ever ask for. She wondered to herself how a man could be so creative, sweet and sharing, but be so evil at the same time.

Nick was really showing Tammy an example of what could happen to her when he had the dead bodies brought around so she could see the bodies disappear. Which she did get the message. Nick had bought his hogs years before for the purpose of getting rid of bodies, which the hogs had gotten rid of plenty. Nick had bought this mansion on the farm because it was always the way he wanted to retire, which was on a farm raising his own meat and growing his own vegetables along with fruits. He had so many animals that it was crazy. He had a twenty-four hour on call farmer. Though the farmer was always there twelve hours every day anyway, the on-call part was just another clause Nick had put in the farmers contract. Nick was in the process of starting to raise Kobe beef, which was a high-quality meat usually imported from Japan. His hopes was to be able to supply grocery stores in the black community with their meat one day for a cheap price. He wanted the grocery stores in the black community to have Kobe beef because he felt black people deserved high-quality meat like anyone else.

Nick was far from retirement, but he still wanted his house on the farm. It's where he found his peace at. He never wanted to bring Sasha's mother to his domain, but he knew no one else knew about it so he figured it was the best idea. He knew there was nothing she could see through the windows so she would never know where she came from after he dropped her back off at home. After all he just wanted to spend time with his son, he just went about seeing his son the only way he knew, which was the gangster way.

Drea came up with the idea to go to Tonya's house to see if they could get any information from her of any kind. Drea and Sasha knocked on the door, as soon as Tonya answered Sasha grabbed her by the neck and welcomed herself and Drea into her home. The rest of the crew sat in Eric's Escalade as lookouts to make sure nothing went wrong outside. They got in and interrogated Tonya to the fullest. At first Tonya acted like they were a joke, then Sasha hit her with a hard-right fist. After that Tonya seen it was real and told them he never told her anything about a kidnapping. She did say he was very upset with Sasha though. They asked her about locations she had been to with him, but the best she could say was that he took her to a house in the Eagle Creek area of Indianapolis. After they felt she was telling the truth they took her phone and headed out the door.

Before shutting the door Drea looked back and said, "bitch you'll be making a big mistake if you tell him or anyone else that this happened. You remember how I beat your ass the other day, this time I will kill you, sneaky slut bitch."

Sasha and the crew were mounted up. Sasha had on old army fatigues and had her handgun from Drea. The rest of the crew were in combat mode themselves.

They were determined to find Sasha's mother and child even without the police. Sasha had an idea on how to find them but didn't know if it would work. She looked around her mother's house for her mother's phone and once she seen it wasn't there, she figured she could trace it by location. Once she tried it said the location was undetermined, but she was working to see if there was any way she could go around it. She kept searching with no success, then she tried another way. She selected "last location" instead of "location" then she got a better result. It said the last location was in Greencastle, Indiana. She told the crew what she came up with, and Eric hit the gas headed for Greencastle, Indiana.

They arrived at the last location detected by the phone. The location was a strip mall. Sasha quickly surveyed the stores. Once she seen the drug store for some reason, she felt they were close to where her mother and her child were located. She doubted that Nick would harm her mother and child, and if that was the case then he would have stopped to get some things they would need. They then rode around the country city of Greencastle looking for any clue that would lead them to her mother and child. Then Sarah asked Sasha if she tried to look up the location of Nick's phone. Everyone looked at Sarah and said it was a very good idea to look up his location.

Once Sasha checked the location on Nick's phone, it read that the location was in route at a high speed. The location was ten miles away and traveling even further by the second. The women said they wanted to try to catch up to the target, but Eric told them that was close to impossible to do. Nick had totally slipped up by having his location active on his phone. Eric told the rest of them he felt Sasha's mother and son were in the area and it would only be so long before Nick would come back. The women didn't like the sound of it, but still agreed to stay in the area to see if Nick would come back any time soon.

Sasha turned on her automatic alert so they would be alerted if he came within fifteen miles of them. They went to grab snacks and waited in the parking lot of the strip mall to see what the results would be. As they sat there waiting, Tonya's phone started to ring. That's when Sasha and Drea gave each other a high five. They took her phone for a reason and it was a good idea, since it was Nick now calling Tonya's phone. They didn't know what to do at this time, then Eric took the phone and answered the phone himself. He answered and to Nick's surprise it was a man answering Tonya's phone. Eric told him to not call his wife's phone again. Nick played it off and acted like he was a telemarketer. They exchanged a few words and hung up the phone.

Nick hung up the phone and was mad about the call he just made. He planned on going to Tonya's house to have sex with her, but now his plans were altered. He tried calling a few other women he knew but came up short with all of them as well. He started cussing to himself and got off on the next exit. He turned around and headed back to where he started. Nick was no stranger to pleasing himself as he had to do for many years in prison, so he figured he would just watch porn and jack off for the night.

Sasha, Eric and Valarie were the only ones up when the alert went off that Nick was within fifteen miles of them. They sat in the parking lot patiently as the target got closer and closer. As the target got within four miles of them, it changed directions and headed another way. Eric then pulled off in the direction the target was headed. He got to a four way stop sign and signaled to go left. They turned left onto a dark street that seemed like a world of its own. That's when they lost signal and could only pick up the last location, which was a little less than three miles away.

As they approached the last location, they were still in the middle of nowhere. From there they just had to guess where to go, which was a headache because it was only farmland in the area. As they traveled to an unknown location Sasha's phone began to ring. To her surprise, it was Nick calling her. She answered the phone after the second ring. Nick told her that he didn't want to hurt her mother, but he would if he had to. He told her that he wanted her to sign over the rights to their son or he would have to do what he had to do. Sasha told him she wouldn't sign over her rights under any circumstance and started to cry as she still talked to him. He then told her that she must have thought he was some type of game and hung up the phone.

Eric continued to drive north on the road they were on. That's when they pulled up to something different from anything else, they had seen on this road. They pulled up to what looked like an estate. The land was gated off for miles. The thing is that this was no ordinary gate. It was cream colored bricks that blocked you from being able to view anything on the other side of it. Sasha knew Nick had a taste for flashy expensive things, so in her mind she felt her mother and son were being held inside those brick walls. That's when she told Eric, she felt they needed to park to figure out what was inside the gates or call the police to figure it out. Everyone chose to see what was inside the brick walls themselves because they figured the police would bring too much attention.

Eric parked his SUV some miles down the road for them to get out and walk to the destination, they didn't want Nick to happen to leave and see a stray vehicle. It was dark outside and there were no streetlights at all. Once they got up to the wall, they seen it would be harder than they thought to get inside or look inside. They could hear what sounded like animals inside. This took them by surprise because from the looks of the wall it didn't look to be somewhere to farm at. They just continued their mission to see if there was any way to look inside. That's when they approached a hill. The center of the hill sat about three fourths up the wall. They all went up and what they seen inside was amazing. There was what looked like a mansion in the middle of a bunch of cattle. Though the house was about a mile and a half ahead of them, they still had no choice but to try to make it there to see what was inside. The crew quietly talked amongst each other and concluded that they would jump the wall and just hope no alarms would go off. They all made sure their guns were secured inside their holsters and jumped the wall.

Nick woke Sasha's mother up telling her that her daughter didn't care about her. He went on and on lying about things Sasha was supposed to had told him about her. She didn't believe him by a long shot, and she continued to tell him that until he got mad. The baby was in the room sound asleep which was good for what was about to unfold. Before you knew it, Nick was snatching off her clothes while choking her and carrying her to the dining area. Sasha's mother had a beautiful shape on her and to be an older woman she was built better than Sasha and many other young women. Nick stared at her golden nipples until he began to suck on them. Sasha's mother started to cry and begged him to stop as he laid her on the floor. He then went down and ate her pussy until her legs locked up like she was enjoying him licking on her, which made him smile. He licked her asshole and did every other freaky thing he could think of to do to her. All the while she just cried and begged him to stop. That's when he grabbed her by her hair, bent her down and started to hit her from the back. Though it looked to be very romantic, Tammy was being raped by her son in law.

As the crew got over the gate they looked and still seen they had far to go. They had to go through many animals, mud, and animal wastes on the way to see what they could see inside the mansion. There were no motion sensors and that was the only good thing they had going for themselves considering they had to go through a maze to even figure out how to get inside. There were many windows on the house so they figured they would peek in whenever they could.

Sasha could hear moaning when she approached a window but could also hear crying at the same time. She realized it was her mother's voice begging whoever it was to stop, but the sounds of the smacks from Nick pounding her mother from the back got louder and louder, then faster and faster. That's when she went around to get a better view and what she seen made her break out in tears instantly. Nick was behind her mother hitting it from the back and from the looks of it he was really enjoying himself. Sasha pulled out her gun and began to shoot through the window. She had a pretty good aim because her father taught her how to shoot in her high school years, but on this night her mind was too all over the place to hit any target.

The bad thing is that Sasha just didn't get there soon enough to save her mother from being raped. Nick really had time to enjoy himself with her mother. He came in Tammy four times and had time to perform oral sex on her several times. Nick tried to force Tammy to give him head, but she wouldn't agree with

169

him no matter what, even after he offered her money. He admired her perfect shape and showed he did by putting hickeys on every part of her body that he could. He even sucked on her cheeks as tears rolled down her face, and while she was still begging him to stop. Nick tried to do any and everything he could to get Tammy to say she liked what he was doing or get a pleasurable moan out of her, but what he didn't know is that if it was up to her she would have died first. Yet and still that didn't stop Nick from trying, nor from exploring every part of her body.

Nick ran through the house naked ducking for cover. Sasha ran to her mother to hold her then went to fetch her trail of clothes to redress her. Her mother cried in her arms like a baby and that's when Sasha asked where Jamal was at. By this time, Nick was being chased by the rest of the crew, but they came up empty. Nick ran in the garage, which looked like a house itself and jumped on a four-wheeler. The garage door opened and before you knew it, he was speeding out on the four-wheeler and going into an underground tunnel. They were able to let a few shots off at Nick, but the entrance to the tunnel closed as they fired. Once the entrance to the tunnel closed, they seen it looked just like another part of the driveway, which made it a hidden tunnel. Sarah called the police from her phone as everyone else stood there with guns in their hands. To their surprise no one else was in the house. The only reason no one else was there is because Nick wanted time alone with Sasha's mom and that's what he got.

No one could believe what had just happened. It was like Nick had a plan for everything that came his way. Though he did lay back and feel comfortable in this house, he kept an escape route just in case. What Sasha didn't know is that even in their Geist house, Nick had a hidden passage to get under ground and come up on the other side of town if he wanted to. Nick put time and thought into everything he did, which is why he was so successful in doing wrong for so many years.

By the time the police arrived, Nick was coming up from the tunnel and headed the other direction. He had a cocaine white Porsche SUV waiting on him on the other side of the tunnel. The police went in and searched everything in the house. They came up with guns, drugs and money. They found many different identification cards that Nick used, and they were getting closer to catching him. Nick had been a fugitive for so long that even the director of the FBI flew out to Greencastle to investigate. The rape unit took Sasha's mother to the hospital, while the police added a rape case to Nick's packet. At this time the director said Nick was too dangerous and he wanted to air the story about him on the news. They had all the evidence they needed to hold him but catching him they knew would be a hard task. Nick knew they would be on him and he had a plan for them as he always did.

CHAPTER 9

Sasha's mother was able to go home from the hospital after two weeks, but only to be hurt with more bad news. Nick was still on the loose and she was pregnant by him. This news made her and Sasha weep, but the tears on Sasha's face were tears of anger. They came from a family that didn't believe in abortions, so aborting the baby was not an option. They sat talking to each other for hours wondering why this was happening to them. After all they felt like they lived there lives right, so they just wondered what God was trying to get them to see. It was hurtful, painful, and disturbing to them both. They wanted justice for what Nick had done to their lives and that was the bottom line.

Over the next few weeks Sasha was still going to work and to her group sessions with Eric. Although she didn't have a lot of money she was still getting back to her normal self. With the help of Drea, Rebecca, Valarie, Sarah and Eric, she was getting to stable grounds, at least mentally. Her son was still her heart and after the kidnapping she made sure he was safe every time she left his presence. She got her a lifetime gun permit and carried a gun everywhere she went, even to the shower. She was determined to make it and she had the heart to never give up.

Meanwhile, Nick was ducked off in Mexico living life to the fullest. He had the money, the power, and the Mexican cartel behind him. All his freakish desires were met as he had many Mexican women living with him and doing what he said. They snorted coke and freaked all day. He still had several people running his drugs and businesses in the United States, so money was still no problem for him. He was even richer in Mexico because American dollars could buy more in Mexico than in the United States. He vowed to make Sasha suffer even more and was just waiting for his opportunity to bring more pain to her.

Sarah and Valarie really worried about Sasha. They had been through so much pain but were experienced in life enough to know how to get over it.

They knew Nick was Sasha's first love, so they knew it would be a while before she healed. Plus, her circumstances were way worse than theirs had ever been. All they knew is that they would be there for her no matter what and she was a little sister to them in their eyes.

While Sarah and Valarie were there for Sasha, they were still weak themselves. The only person who was keeping them from being back in their same situations was Eric. They both still had conversations with their exes, but only Sarah was considering taking her ex back, which she secretly did. She believed the words of her ex-husband and let him come back home. He immediately started to dominate her again. Since no one knew she was back with him, no one could tell her to leave him alone. Sarah eventually quit going to her meetings and told the group to let her be for a while so she could sort out some life issues.

Things were getting back to as normal as they could be under the circumstances. Everyone was just doing their own thing, trying to get better in life, but at the same time worrying about Sarah. Sarah was one of the prettiest women you could find. She stood about five foot one and had a body like a model. She was Caucasian, but everyone always told her she was strapped like a black woman. She was very sweet and would do whatever she could for anybody, even a stranger. When she first met her husband, she was at the top of her game. He seen a way to make money from her body without her even knowing and took advantage of it. He was jealous of all the attention she got from other men, he felt she was too friendly with them. That's when all the abuse started. Then in his mind he thought she was cheating, so he figured if she was going to be a hoe then she would be a hoe for him. Though Sarah never cheated on him or thought about cheating on him.

After getting Sarah back Tim felt he had lost control of her because she was gone for so long. He hated the fact that she read Eric's book and was going to his battered women meetings. Once he influenced her to quit talking to everyone at the group, he felt he had the old Sarah back. Then the day came that she didn't come back from work on time. Tim paced the floor cussing to himself, throwing tables and even threw all the food in the refrigerator onto the kitchen floor. As soon as Sarah pulled up, he was out the door and running up to her car. He flung her car door opened, grabbed her out by the neck and carried her into the house.

Once they were in the house, he threw her on the floor, jumped on top of her and began to beat her. Sarah cried begging him to leave her alone, but he was in so much rage that he couldn't even hear her. When she went back to Tim, she knew what the possibilities were with him. She just didn't know that he was even more on edge than before because he hated that she was letting a black man influence her. Tim hated Eric and wanted to kick his ass but knew he couldn't.

Tim then told her, "bitch, now I'm not going to drug you, you're going to willingly sell some pussy for me."

That's when Sarah tried to fight back and was knocked to the floor again. She was bleeding from her nose and mouth. Tim went in the room and got the bed ready for her to be raped by various unknown men. He tied her up with her butt still tooted in the air and started to make phone calls. Before you knew it, about seven guys were knocking at the door. They all had sex with Sarah. After a while she just stopped crying and took the pain and humiliation. She just didn't know that her crying while having sex was most of these men weird fetishes. After hours of being raped the traffic finally calmed down.

Tim then told her to never disobey him again and untied her. He told her to go cook for him and clean herself up. Sarah went into the restroom and turned on the shower. She silently called Sasha and told her what had happened. Sarah asked Sasha to not come over, but to please let her stay at her mother's house with her once she got out of the house with Tim. Sasha didn't listen and went to Sarah's house anyway. Sarah was in the shower when she heard the doorbell ring. Soon after she heard scuffling. Then she could hear Tim say, "bitch, I'm a sell your ass too." Tim then slapped Sasha to the ground. As he went to get on top of her, he was shot. Sasha pulled her gun from her side and shot Tim four times.

Sarah came out the restroom still naked and ran to hold Sasha. She looked at Tim and spit on him. Within minutes they could hear police sirens coming their way, Tim was still breathing and trying to get the strength to attack Sasha and Sarah some more. Sasha had shot him in both legs, the arm and grazed his neck. Sasha was very surprised at how calm she was after shooting someone, for some reason it made her feel like she had the power. The police asked Sasha and Sarah a few questions and said they would be on their way out after looking at a few things around the house. Sarah told the cops what happened from the beginning to the end with her ex-husband, Tim. The police then took Tim to Wishard hospital and cuffed him to the bed, letting him know he was going to jail after his wounds were healed.

Once the word got out to Drea about what had just happened, she hurried to call Sasha. Sasha told her she was fine, and Sarah was the one who needed to be worried about. Sarah had to go to the hospital to do a rape exam. So many men had sex with her that her private part was wide opened. They could tell she had also been penetrated in her butt. Sasha was by her side the whole time and Sarah told her that she would make Tim pay this time. The detectives told Sarah that they would prosecute even the men who paid to have sex with her. The police confiscated Tim's phone and were able to find out every man who had gone to Sarah's house. Sarah told them about the video tapes Tim had of her also. After a search of the residence, detectives were able to find all the evidence they needed to charge

Tim with human trafficking, rape, confinement, battery and many other charges.

The news of Sasha shooting someone traveled quick. So, quick that the word even got to Nick while he was in Mexico. Nick got very angry when he was able to watch it on the news. He wanted Sasha to be suffering, but she didn't seem to be suffering while doing a news interview. Sasha explained her own personal situation during the interview as well. Her and Sarah's whole support group was on the news with them. That's when Nick saw Eric and got even more angry. He knew Eric from the streets and knew he had turned his life around but was mad about him being around Sasha. Especially being that Eric was holding Sasha every time she was ready to shed a tear. This brought rage to Nick's heart and made him put a hit out on Eric. Nick put a two hundred and fifty-thousand-dollar bounty on Eric's head. The only thing Nick didn't know is that Eric still had ties to the streets as well.

Sarah recovered and was out the hospital in seven days. She went to stay with Sasha and her mom until she felt comfortable enough to go home. Everything in her house, including the house was hers. Tim came into her life with his own money, but Sarah made him even more of a man and Tim still treated her like nothing. She was beyond the phase of trying to figure things out, instead she focused on prosecuting him. Her job told her to take a few weeks off, but she chose to go back anyway. Sarah was a senior saleswoman for H.H. Gregg and made a nice wage of money in her position, plus she loved her line of work. Instead of sitting around thinking about things, she chose to go to work and do what she loved to do.

Eric didn't like the fact that Sarah wanted to go back to work so soon. He knew Sarah wanted to stay busy to keep her mind off Tim, but knew it wasn't healthy for her to do. Eric tried to explain to all the ladies in his group that once they could get comfortable by themselves not doing anything, they were well on their way to recovery. The thing he tried to get them to understand is that no matter what they couldn't work themselves to death trying to keep their minds off their situations. Instead he wanted them to build up their self-confidence alone, so they would never have to depend on anyone to feel whole. That way if they were to ever be done wrong again. They would be strong enough to leave the man and even without a replacement of some sort, they would still be able to stand on their decision alone. Eric knew from his years of leading groups that most women stayed in abusive relationships because they didn't want to be alone.

Sasha was at work about to go on lunch break when a lady who was a regular at the Mc Donald's asked her if she could sit with her for lunch. Sasha was familiar with her, so she said yes. The lady's name was Tajuanda. She was a woman who had been through a lot herself, but you would never be able to tell by the way she walked with her head held so high. Tajuanda was familiar with Sasha's situation because she was also in Eric's meeting with her, though Sasha never seen her. Tajuanda had been through hell and back with her ex and now she was the owner of a real estate company. All she sold was upscale houses that cost hundreds of thousands, if not millions. She wanted to teach Sasha the real estate game because she seen potential in her. She seen how Sasha was with people and knew what Sasha had been through. She knew that if Sasha could hide all her pain behind a smile while treating her customers with the genuine respect she did, she would be good to have on her team.

Sasha and Tajuanda sat at the table, both with crispy chicken salads and ice teas sweetened with Splenda. Tajuanda introduced herself and told Sasha that she seen her at Eric's meetings. Sasha was caught by surprise, but happy that Tajuanda took notice into her. Tajuanda told her some of the things she went through and how she overcame it. Then told her that she wanted to train her and make her a part of Straight Thang Realty. She told Sasha the potential commission checks she could make on top of her yearly salary. Plus told her if she put in a two weeks' notice at Mc Donald's right away, she would give her a fifteen-thousand-dollar sign on bonus. The sign on bonus was for Sasha to stay above ground on bills and things like that until she got her first check. Tajuanda was a black woman with power and wanted to uplift every woman she could, no matter their race, but it was only certain women she felt had the attitude to make it in the real estate industry and Sasha was one of them.

After discussing many details, Sasha agreed to put in her two-week notice. Tajuanda walked back out the door of Mc Donald's with a smile on her face. She had just put another woman on her team and knew it would change Sasha's life for the better. Tajuanda prided herself on building strong women. She was in her forties and was like a mother figure to many young women and some older women too. She only had seven other women on her team because she chose her team wisely, but they were all making big money and that's all that mattered to her. She also turned many other women onto money but sent them to other business owners she knew.

Over the next couple months Sasha was training to become the best real estate agent she could become. She studied day in and day out. She even adjusted her diet to a healthier one that she thought would help her retain memory. When she left Nick's house, she had nothing, not even clothes, but now she was sitting with over seventeen thousand dollars in her bank account. She had moved out of her mother's house and into her own apartment in a north side suburb of Indianapolis called Fishers. Life had gotten better for her and was getting even better by the minute.

Sasha's mother was dealing with a high-risk pregnancy due to her age. She didn't even want to leave the house. She felt very embarrassed and wanted to go against her beliefs of abortion and have one, but her preacher persuaded her to do otherwise. He told her to pray on it and God would send her in the right direction. He let her know that the baby had nothing to do with what was going on and deserved a chance to be on the earth. She didn't feel that way at all, but she continued to pray on it and keep going with her pregnancy. Though she never had a bad feeling about anyone in life, she wanted to kill Nick with her own bare hands. She made a promise to herself that she would never let Nick see the baby and she would be there every day of his trial when the police found him to make sure they found him guilty.

Eric caught word that Nick had a bounty on his head. Being that Eric used to extort Nick he knew Nick's strengths and weaknesses. In no way, could Eric take this lightly, so he went to the streets. He was his own man and wouldn't mention a word of it to none of the ladies. Eric went to the main hoods in Indianapolis where he felt he could find the whereabouts of Nick. He traveled to Haughville, Bright Wood, and a neighborhood off fortieth and Boulevard, in Indianapolis. While talking to one of his buddies from

Bright Wood he found out Nick was hiding in Mexico. Eric's next move was to go to Mexico. Many would have been scared to take on such a mission against a man in the cartel, but they all knew Eric from his previous life and had much respect for him. He could have been the big man in Indianapolis way before Nick, but after going to federal prison, he came out with a different mindset to do right and that's what he had done. Under any circumstance, he would defend his life though, and that's what he was setting out to do.

Over the next couple days Eric was preparing to go to Mexico with the intentions to find and kill Nick. He talked to two guys he still trusted in Indianapolis, a guy by the name of Lil Art from Boulevard and a guy named D-Lo from Haughville. They informed him about all the soldiers Nick still had in Indianapolis and the roles they played. They told him of all the talk and possible people who were trying to collect on the bounty. They told him they would go with him as Nick had done them dirty too, but Eric was determined to handle his own dirty work.

By the end of the night Drea had caught word of the bounty on Eric's head and called him immediately. He told her that it was true, but it would be handled accordingly. Drea knew Eric didn't play no games in the streets, but she also knew he had lost a lot of his power because he had been out the game so long. She told him she needed to meet with him as soon as possible and had a solid plan to get Nick without him having to put his life at risk. After a lot of persuading, Eric agreed to meet with Drea. She didn't tell him she would bring Sasha along, but that was her plan.

Sasha completed her test to become a real estate agent in a very powerful way. She passed her test with one hundred percent, not one wrong answer. She did so good that even Tajuanda herself applauded her. Tajuanda and the rest of the women in her crew had a meeting. This made the other women look up to Tajuanda even more because she had hand-picked a woman who passed the test with a perfect score. Though this was just the beginning, it was still a very good look. Tajuanda introduced Sasha to the team with a big bang. They rented out a hall, invited many people and partied like there was no tomorrow. Sasha was having the time of her life. They informed her that the following morning she would be going straight into the real estate field as an agent and property manager supervisor.

Sasha woke up the next morning. She first got herself and her son together. After dropping her son off she headed to meet with Sarah, Rebecca and Valarie for breakfast. They met up at a restaurant called IHOP where they all indulged in high calorie meals as a celebration for Sasha. None of the ladies could make it to the party the night before, but they sure made up for it. Sasha knew that after breakfast she would be going into work with her mind set on selling a house or maybe even more than one. She stayed optimistic about the situation. For the first time since her split with Nick she felt like she could take on the world again.

Sasha got into her new office and was very surprised and happy with the office size, decorations, and features that Tajuanda had chosen for her. Her office was big enough to fit her whole apartment inside of it, along with top notch furniture in it to fill the space. It had its own loft and sat on the twenty seventh floor of a building located at "Keystone at the Crossings" in Indianapolis. Her company car, which she could take home with her and use at her own leisure was a customized hot pink Range Rover. She was in the big leagues now and didn't even know it. Seemed that no sooner than she sat at her desk her phone started to ring. When she answered, it was someone looking to buy a house.

Drea was sitting there waiting on Sasha to pull up to get her. Sasha didn't know what was going on, but knew it was important and urgent. Once Drea was in the Range Rover she began to tell Sasha about what was going on. Sasha immediately told her that she just wanted to be done with the whole Nick situation. Drea warned her that if she didn't face it, Nick would haunt her for the rest of her life. She also let her know that the plan she had wouldn't put anyone at risk. Sasha still refused to go along with the plan. Drea was upset but understood where Sasha was coming from. She knew that Sasha was just getting started in life and knew nothing about the streets, but still assured Sasha that she had her back. Sasha still went to the meeting with Drea to show her support for Eric though.

CHAPTER 10

Sasha was out with her clients letting them see the many houses they could purchase off the market. It was a man his wife and one child. These people seemed to be regular however their pocketbooks were far from regular. They were looking to purchase a house off the market and had over a million dollars to spend. With a budgeting price like that Sasha would earn over a hundred and fifty thousand dollars in commission. Although Sasha was never money hungry, she had her mind on living how she did when Nick came into her life. Nick introduced her to a lifestyle she liked, but she seen what could happen if she didn't buy the lifestyle for herself. Now she worked hard to bring that lifestyle to fruition for herself and her son, on her own. In some type of way, Nick turned her into a money go getter.

After taking her clients out and giving them many options to choose from, Sasha headed back to her office. To her surprise, Tajuanda had even more clients for her. Also, Sasha had picked up a client on her own, it was her old manager from Nordstrom. Mr. Jackson heard about Sasha joining real estate through the grape vine and was on the market to purchase a house, so he chose to use her as his agent. In just one day, Sasha had picked up nine potential buyers.

With all the good going on in Sasha's life, she couldn't afford to take another fall. Drea had a plan to lure Nick back to Indianapolis. She wanted Sasha to just stay silent and do her thang but wanted Eric to put a bounty back out on Nick's head and was going to have her cousins start robbing all of Nick's workers. She knew in the back of her mind that Nick would come back to Indy if his money started to take a loss in the Indy streets. She had her mind set on Nick playing a dirty game, so she was going to play a dirty game right along with him. Plus, with Nick having her shot at, she knew she was in the loop too and wanted him to be dead before someone she loved or cared for ended up dead. This plan sounded good to Eric and he told her he couldn't have made a cleverer plan himself. Now it was time for Drea and Eric to play the game the way Nick wanted to play it, which was dirty and straight down to business. Eric went out to the Indy streets and put a six-hundred-thousand-dollar bounty on Nick's head. Eric and Drea warned Sasha to watch her back and just stay out of the loop.

Four days had passed, and Sasha was already closing on a one point eight-million-dollar house. She almost fainted when she totaled over two-hundred thousand dollars in commission with a nice bonus included. When she told her mother the news, her mother cried tears of joy. Rebecca, Sarah, Valarie and Drea were all in awe. They were happy for her and asked about getting into real estate themselves, seeing a check like Sasha's sparked all their interests. Not only had Sasha closed on a house in her first week, but she was looking to close on two more homes the next day. This was the break anyone would have loved to have in life, especially Sasha at this time. She wanted to persuade her mother into leaving her house and moving to one that Nick wouldn't know. Then as a real estate agent she could put her mother's house back on the market herself. For once in life Sasha finally felt like she earned something on her own. She thanked Tajuanda so much for seeing potential in her. She felt God had sent Tajuanda into her life for a reason, and it wasn't just about money. Tajuanda was building her up mentally as well.

One of Drea's cousins named Damo pulled up to one of Nick's workers. As soon as he asked Damo what he wanted thinking he wanted crack, Damo put the gun on him and went in his pockets. After Damo took his money, gun, and drugs, he started to beat him with his pistol. Damo told him to tell his boss that Eric sent him, and that Eric was going to take back over the streets of Indianapolis. Damo then spit on him and went on about his way. While Damo was robbing one of the workers on the east side, another one of Drea's cousins named Turk was robbing one on the west side. In all, eight of Nick's houses were being robbed at the same time. This was going to send a big message to Nick and let him know that Eric wasn't scared of him in the least bit.

Sasha told Eric that she would give up one hundred thousand dollars towards Nick getting killed if someone did find him and kill him. So far it was looking ugly for Nick, he put money on the wrong man's head. The only problem at hand for Eric was that Nick had soldiers all around the United States and in Mexico, so he had no idea which direction they would come from, nor did he know the color they would be. Eric was no stranger to the streets though and watched his back very carefully even after changing his life. One thing for sure was that this would be a battle for both men.

At one of Nick's trap houses in Bright Wood one of his soldiers wouldn't give in to one of the robbers, so the robber ended up having to kill him. There was news crews all around Indianapolis, at the same time. It seemed like as soon as one unit was dispatched to one side of town, there was another unit going to either the same side of town or the other side of town. Eric knew this method would send a strong message to Nick; he learned this method from doing federal prison time. While Eric was in prison, when he went to war with his crew, they set it off in all the dorms in the prison at the same time, so he figured he would use the same method while on the streets. While the news station was in Haughville at a crime scene, you could hear even more gunshots being fired off. Drea mentioned an idea to Eric and he went on with it, but he knew he wouldn't have been able to go to war the way he was without Drea's family. Eric thought about how grateful he was for Drea's idea to lure Nick back to Indy and her soldiers. They just wanted Nick dead and that was the bottom line, but Nick wanted them dead too.

So far it was going down in Indianapolis. Police sirens everywhere! Nick got the message while still in Mexico. He was so mad that he bit his own bottom lip until it started bleeding. Nick was devastated by what was going on. Out of his whole career in the streets, he had never been hit that hard. Nick hated to feel outsmarted and, on this occasion, he was more than outsmarted, he was also caught off guard. No one would ever think to go against him in a way like this, but it was happening now, and he knew they meant business.

Nick after all used to give Eric a weekly fee to keep him from robbing him and taking everything back in the day. It was just that when Eric went back to prison, Nick got a powerful connect on drugs and gained power. In no way, would Eric ever back down from a battle though especially when his life was on the line. Nick also heard about the bounty on his head for six hundred thousand dollars, but thought it was a joke until everything else popped off in Indianapolis. Eric even talked to some of his Mexicans down in Mexico to try to get them to find Nick and kill him. So far Eric was ahead of Nick and started off the war with the help of Drea.

Nick was in Mexico with soldiers trying to get a counterattack planned. Being that he didn't know anything about Eric's whereabouts it would be hard to attack him. He foamed at the mouth trying to figure out what to do. One thing about Nick is that he always liked to feel superior, but Eric was making him look like a victim. His Indianapolis soldiers now looked sweeter than bear meat to all the other drug organizations around town. In just one day, over one hundred thousand dollars of Nick's profit had been lost and he didn't like it. He knew he had to do something, and knew he had to do it fast. He sat at the round table with his soldiers contemplating a plan.

While all this was going on Tim was in the hospital being released to the Indianapolis Police Department. Tim would not cooperate with detectives at all. He cussed them out and tried to fight them every chance he got. He made phone calls and the reason for all the phone calls he made, was to get someone to go murder Sarah and Sasha. Once he did get in the county jail, he wasn't so aggressive towards anyone. He was only the big bad wolf when it came to women. When it came to other men, he was just a punk. One guy noticed who he was and just sat back plotting on him. He knew Tim had quite a bit of money and was a punk, so he had plans of extorting Tim for commissary. As soon as commissary day came around Tim was robbed and beat up for his commissary. The men he was in the block with didn't like woman beaters and showed it by their actions. Tim tried to leave the block telling the guards he was in fear of his life and the guards laughed at him then let the door slam in his face.

Sasha was watching TV when a news alert came on the screen. They had a headline story about Nick. They said he was the one responsible for the war going on in Indianapolis. They considered him armed and dangerous. They warned that if anyone was to see him to never approach him, but to keep him in sight and alert the FBI immediately. The news just didn't know that Nick was the victim in this situation, looking for a way to attack back. Drea threw the pitch to lure Nick back to Indy and Eric plotted the attacks and so far, the plan was going better than expected. She knew before long Nick would be back in the Indy area, but when he did come back not only were the street soldiers going to be on him, the police would be on him as well. Sasha knew the plan and was happy to know that sooner than later Nick would be taken down.

Sarah was having a bad day at work. She was worried that her life was in danger because she heard about the threats Tim had made towards her life. The only thing that kept her from worrying was that she had a support team who would do whatever they needed to do to keep her safe. Tim just didn't know who he was going up against. Sarah was a pawn on the chess board to Tim, but he didn't know the enforcement behind her made her the queen of the board. Tim was facing over two hundred years in prison, so Sarah should have been the least of his worries. Being that the DA's office had all the evidence they needed to convict him. Even if he was to have Sarah killed, he would still be convicted. Sarah just went on with her day trying not to worry about Tim.

Meanwhile, Valarie was opening her new beauty salon. This time she was determined to not let another man come in and crash what she had worked so hard to build. She was really a good woman at heart and easy to get over on. All a man had to do was come up to her saying the right words and she would fall for it each time. Now that Eric was in the picture things were a lot different. In Eric's book, he outlined every angle a no-good man would come from, not sparing any feelings, instead he was bringing the straight truth in a raw way. Valarie knew that Eric's life was on the line and did everything she could do to keep him alive. The ladies didn't worship Eric, but they did love him to death for the help and encouragement he had given them.

Sasha went into her office the next day and was surprised to see that Mr. Jackson and his newlywed wife were waiting on her in the lobby. They were ready to close on their house. Though it wasn't over a million-dollar home like the first one she sold it was still over a three hundred-thousand-dollar home, so she would still get a nice commission check from the sale. Things were really falling into place for Sasha. She had never had over six thousand dollars in her bank account at once before meeting Nick, but now she was sitting on over two hundred thousand dollars and still counting. She remembered the words her father told her in her teenage years and that was that "some people are a lesson and some people are a blessing in your life." Nick's lesson in her life turned out to be a blessing, but she was still going through a hard ass lesson. Tajuanda told her she would make her a millionaire and she was well on the way to becoming one. Sasha was happy with herself, but she knew she couldn't really enjoy her accomplishments until Nick was either dead or in prison.

As the first couple weeks of Sasha's career as a real estate agent ended, she had closed on nine houses. Tajuanda told her in the beginning that the real estate game had ups and downs. That's why Tajuanda had formed a plan for her whole team to still eat even through the real estate drought that happens to every real estate agent. Tajuanda had purchased seventeen apartment complexes, which brought in over twenty million a year in profit. Plus, her real estate company owned over one hundred rental houses. With those secured incomes coming in she paid her whole team over an eighty-thousand-dollar a year salary. Working with Tajuanda was more like a building experience for anyone. She made sure her whole team worked on their credit scores and everything while working for her. Being that Tajuanda started Straight Thang Realty from being homeless, she knew the ropes when it came to person going from nothing to something. The money was flowing in for them all, but without the right mindset Tajuanda warned them that the ship would sink, so she kept them on game. Tajuanda didn't just want her team to be workers, she wanted them in a position to either invest in part of her company or start their own. She named her firm Straight Thang Realty because she wanted her whole team to be straight thang, which was a term used in Indy for being one hundred percent on point and bossed up.

While things were going good for Sasha, they were also going good for Drea. Drea was starting her own make up and nail salon. While at the same time starting a flower shop. Drea was big on beauty and loved to make others look beautiful. Drea thought she would never leave Nordstrom, but with the way things were going she knew she was well on her way to becoming an independent successful business owner. She was just waiting on her time to shine and not trying to rush things. She didn't want to quit her job until she knew her businesses were well established.

Rebecca and Nathan were still together, but Rebecca didn't bring him around Sasha much because he still worked for Nick. It was just a conflict of interest that she knew could bring problems to their friendship. No one knew how Nathan got his orders on what to do with Nick's enterprise, but the enterprise continued to grow in Nick's absence. Nathan didn't like working for Nick under the circumstances of what happened with Sasha, but the money was too good for him to turn his back on the enterprise. He told Rebecca he would get the money while he could, knowing it wouldn't last forever.

Nick had a solid foundation when it came to the many businesses he owned. No matter what the Feds tried to do they couldn't touch his companies, which they tried to do for many years. He still had his wife in California, whose name was on most companies, but after she seen him on the FBI's most wanted, she was starting to stray away so she could save what she did have left. She loved Nick but didn't love him enough to go to prison for him or lose what she had already built on her own. For the time being she was a sitting duck, but she had a plan for that too. Nick was smart enough to know not to give her too much information, knowing that she would tell if pushed enough by detectives. Even though Nick didn't tell Kim much, she was still determined to find out some things on her own. She now knew she was married to an alias instead of a man.

CHAPTER 11

Things calmed down in Indianapolis over the weeks, but smoke was still in the air. Nick started his operation back up and was making up for the many losses he had taken. Just when he thought things were back on stable grounds, Eric hit him with another surprise attack. This time they hit all his houses in Indianapolis again, plus attempted to kill him while he was still in Mexico. Six hundred thousand dollars was too much for another cartel in Mexico to turn down, so they tried to fulfill the hit on Nick. Though it was unsuccessful, it let Nick know he wasn't untouchable and that the doors were starting to close in on him. Eric made sure to give the other Mexican cartel a hundred thousand dollars for the close attempt, which satisfied them enough to keep trying.

Nick woke up the morning he was almost killed by the other cartel, doing his normal daily chores, but something was different. On this day, the newspaper boy brought the newspaper to his door instead of throwing it like he normally did. Nick was a man who made the same moves at the same times every day, so anything out of the ordinary he would notice. When the paper boy came to the door Nick was already prepared for the ambush. There was a sniper sitting yards away that took a shot at Nick before he could duck for cover. Nick barely escaped the shot. After that Nick called his troops and said he was going back to Indianapolis to handle the beef with Eric once and for all. Nick just knew the attempt on his life came from the money Eric had put on his head.

Sasha was in the mode of making money. She got with Rebecca and came up with a plan for them to open a lounge for women in Indianapolis. She wanted to call it the Lady's Lounge, where women paid a monthly membership fee to be a part of the lounge. In the lounge, she wanted to have a bar, a spa, a nail tech, and many other things for women. She figured it would gross enough money to pay the women who worked for them a decent hourly rate. At the same time, she felt they would be able to donate money to a women's shelter in Indianapolis called the Julian Center for Women. Sasha made it a must to help women going through the same thing she was going through, just like Tajuanda was helping her. Sasha had run the idea by Tajuanda and once she got the go ahead from her, she brought the proposition to her best friend. Rebecca was happy and very enthusiastic about the idea. Rebecca told Sasha that they may had come out better than going to college, Sasha told her she felt the same way. Sasha knew that before long she would bring her whole crew into her business, she just had to continue to work hard.

Sasha's mother just couldn't get ahold of herself. She knew she couldn't have a baby and was about to go against what she felt about abortion. Things just weren't adding up for her. Tammy was a woman who had one child and never planned on having another one. Her life was about doing what was right, though she had made mistakes in the past. She figured she would pray and whatever came to her after that, she would stick to it even if it meant having an abortion.

As Nick looked onto the field of soldiers that moved under his command, he said to himself, "that bitch ass nigga is dead."

The look in his eyes said death. The actions he acted upon said murder. In no way was this a game to Nick and he planned to show it. Nick needed to understand that he wasn't the toughest nigga in the world though. Nick had already alerted border patrol that him and fifty others would be coming through before long. After getting into the United States, Nick knew he would be a walking target for police and niggas, but when it came to his money, he didn't give a fuck.

As the Christmas season approached, Sasha looked forward to the New Year's and beyond. She finally got her mother to move out of the house she lived in since Sasha was a child. Sasha found her place to start up her women's lounge and had over four hundred thousand dollars in the bank. She had a promising future ahead of her with the company she worked for. Overall things were going great, even with the thoughts of Nick in the back of her mind. She knew to stay alert, but she wasn't scared of Nick anymore. Jamal made all her worries go away and she thanked God for her son. No matter how much she disliked Nick, she still looked at her son by him as the love of her life. Over the few months that went past, her life had made a huge turnaround and she was very grateful for the turnaround.

The building Sasha picked out for her lounge sat on one of the busiest streets in Indianapolis, a street called 38th street. Right in Drea's neighborhood on a street called Hawthorne. She was also moving forward with opening a car lot that went off income, instead of credit scores. Her mind was fixated on success and success is what she was determined to have. She was once the one who needed everyone to help her mentally, but now she was the one who everyone looked to for mental support. Eric told her daily that she made a difference sooner than any woman he had ever counseled.

Eric sat on Butler Avenue with his own crew. A crew of retired original gangsters that would only move for the right cause. Along with them, Eric had many people who Drea connected him with. Nick was so grimy to everyone that many people were now turning on him for Eric. Nick killed so many people and had so many people killed that he couldn't possibly know who their family members were. Most of the people Eric had riding with him were family members of people who Nick murdered or had murdered, and they had been waiting for retaliation. They just couldn't stand strong on their own. When Eric came, he gave them the confidence they needed to stand up and be men. Nick was coming to surprise Eric, but he was in for a big surprise himself. Drea and Eric knew that interfering with Nick's money, would bring him out of hiding sooner or later, so they just waited patiently and were well prepared. What Nick thought would be a surprise was really part of the plan, he was outsmarted this time.

As Nick was getting in his SUV to leave Mexico, he got orders from the leader of the cartel to stay in Mexico. His reason was that he couldn't risk losing Nick, so he wanted to send someone else in his place so Nick could stay safe. Nick was pissed off about this, because he didn't like no one telling him what to do, but he seen the logic in what his boss was saying. Nick was the cartels main man in the United States, and no one had ever done what Nick had done, so Nick held great value in the cartel. The leader of the cartel would risk many people, but he couldn't risk Nick.

Sarah was getting ready to leave Indianapolis. She was too scared to stay in Indianapolis. Tim scared her to the fullest degree of scaring someone. No matter what anyone said to her she just couldn't get comfortable. She was leaving for Arizona and would only come back to Indy to testify on Tim. She had a job and everything else set up in Arizona to start a new life there. She was leaving just seven days before Christmas, but she felt it was what was needed.

From the outside looking in you would have thought things were going great for Eric, Sasha and the rest of the crew. Sasha had bought everything Nick had bought her and more. Eric continued to go to work and do his meetings with women every day during the week. Drea was now a business owner. Valarie was doing great with the new salon she started up. None of the ladies were burdened with the problem of a no-good man. Things were looking up, but everyone knew they couldn't live to the fullest until Nick was dead, they didn't even want him in prison because he would still have too much power there. Things looked cool from the outside and that's what they wanted it to stay looking like, so once they did strike, no one would see it coming and they would be the least expected.

Christmas day came around! Sasha was with her mother and Jamal at the new house Sasha had bought for her mother. Jamal had more than enough gifts. The gifts he had alone was more than enough to supply four kids put together. Since Tammy went against having an abortion, she was getting a nursery together for her soon to be child. Sasha and her mother just sat there drinking hot chocolate, talking, and watching Jamal open his gifts. They still had a little time left before friends and other family members would start showing up, so they used that time to talk about older holiday memories.

While everyone else was enjoying their Christmas, Nick was plotting. He wanted Eric, Sasha and Drea dead. It seemed like he got more hateful towards them by the minute. First, he only wanted Eric dead, but he kept adding people to the list as he thought about it. Mexico was starting to get hot for him too, so he was planning an escape from there also. He could speak seven different languages fluently, so he figured he would go somewhere where he knew their primary language. For some reason he figured he would end up in Brazil.

Sasha left Jamal with her mother because she planned to go out with Drea and Drea's family for a while. She was heading to her apartment to get changed and freshen up a little bit. She pulled up to her apartment with Mystical "Shake it fast" bumping loud, that was one of her favorite songs since her school days. Even on Christmas she was still alert and aware of her surroundings. She was walking up the walkway to her apartment when someone came out of nowhere trying to snatch her up. A van pulled up waiting on the masked person to put her in the back, but they were in for a big surprise. Sasha retrieved her pistol and shot the person in the mask trying to grab her square in the face and then turned around and started firing at the van. The van sped off but crashed a few yards away in the parking lot. Sasha had even shot the driver too. From an innocent woman to a murderer is what Sasha now was, after being with Nick she had no choice but to protect herself and her family.

Fishers police came to the scene immediately. Neighbors from all around came to see what was going on with Sasha. One neighbor even told her that he had seen a man trying to get into her door with a key. The neighbor said he thought the man was someone she knew because he seen him come out of her apartment before. He told her he had never seen anyone be so bold when committing a crime, so he thought for sure no crime was being committed. The police told her she did the right thing by protecting herself. Sasha told the police everything that had been going on and they felt sorry for her. One officer went in the masked man's pocket and found keys to Sasha's apartment; he then gave Sasha bullets from his car and told her to be careful. The police told Sasha they would always have a patrol car in the apartments. News cameras were all around, but Sasha refused to give an interview, though many neighbors did tell what they saw.

By the time, Sasha's support team showed up, she was ready for combat. Eric and Drea walked up to Sasha and her words were, "I'm out of here and heading to Mexico to kill this son of a bitch myself."

Drea liked seeing the fire in Sasha and knew Sasha was serious but going to Mexico was far too dangerous. They tried talking Sasha out of going, but she wouldn't listen. Sasha called her boss Tajuanda and told her that she needed time off work. Sasha told her that she feared for her life, her son's life, and her mother's life. Tajuanda told her to take off as much time as she needed and to call her if she needed her. When Sasha told her about going to Mexico, Tajuanda told her that she was well connected down there and could help her, though Sasha never told her what she was going for.

Tajuanda was no stranger to danger, nor was she a stranger to Nick. What Sasha didn't know is that Tajuanda helped her because her sister was murdered while being with Nick. Nick threw Tajuanda's sister in front of him to catch a bullet for him, which was a head

shot. Tajuanda's sister had a big stash of Nick's that

Tajuanda found but never returned it to Nick because

he tried to kill her. Nick tried to kill Tajuanda only

because she knew too much information. Eventually

Tajuanda started dating someone Nick knew and Nick

made him beat her continuously, until Tajuanda

eventually killed him.

After Tajuanda killed her boyfriend, she went

homeless because she spent all Nick's stash trying to

please him before she killed him. Nothing was enough

for him though because he did everything Nick told him

to do. From that point on she hated Nick and wouldn't

rest until he was dead. She seen Sasha with Nick one

time and then seen her at the meetings and knew she

had to have been there because of Nick. So, she wanted

to build Sasha in every way so she would be ready for

Nick and she did just that. Sasha was more than ready

and wanted to bring the drama to Nick instead of him

bringing it to her now. The beast unleashed in Sasha, was all a part of Nick's doings so he had to live with it.

Sasha had her game face on and was ready for action. Sasha, Eric and Drea were the ones going on the trip. Tajuanda told Sasha that she lined up for them to have extra security and weapons once they arrived in Mexico. They had a rock-solid plan and had hope that it would go through for them. Nick had to be stopped and, in their eyes, they would have to be the ones who stopped him. There wasn't no turning back now!

CHAPTER 12

For Sasha to had just killed two people a few days ago, she was still very calm. She knew what needed to be done. Her plan was to show a few more houses, make sure Jamal was safe and secured, then head out for Mexico. Nick turned Sasha into a monster, which she really didn't like being that way, but it was necessary to deal with a monster like Nick. She thought back every day about what she could have done to deserve the treatment she was treated with, but knew it was too late to think. What had to be done had to be done and that was the bottom line in her eyes. Eric tried to talk sense into her, but she just couldn't hear it because too many people were starting to die.

Sasha pulled up with her last clients before she was to head off to Mexico that night. It was a million-dollar house in an outside Indianapolis town called Greenwood. Her clients were husband and wife, along with two children. They looked at the house and said it was the house they wanted. Sasha was happy to hear that considering she had already showed them thirteen other houses. After shaking hands, they were on their way out the door when Sasha was knocked off her feet. The so-called wife sent electricity through Sasha with a Taser gun. Within seconds of being shocked with the high voltage Taser gun Sasha was knocked unconscious.

Once Sasha was on the ground the so-called wife and kids left the house leaving the man behind with Sasha. The man taped Sasha up and waited on a dark green extended cargo van to pull in the garage, he then loaded her into the van. Sasha gained consciousness after about thirty minutes only to see she was blind folded, taped up, and held captive. After a long ride the door opened, and she was taken out of the van. They put her on an airplane and on into the sky they traveled. Just that fast Sasha's plan had folded, and she knew she was now on her way to see Nick in Mexico but under his terms, not hers. The weird part is that she was ready to face him once and for all, she had no fears.

Drea called Sasha's phone only to get no answer. Drea knew Sasha couldn't answer the phone sometimes due to work, so she just sat back and waited on her to call back. After waiting over three hours, Drea called Sasha again, but there was still no answer. After the second no answer, Drea started calling around to see if anyone knew where Sasha was at. No one knew! Drea jumped in her car and headed to Sasha's job, but to her surprise she wasn't there. Tajuanda was there and started to look up the last houses Sasha had on her agenda to show. She seen the Greenwood house and they both were out the door headed to Greenwood.

Tajuanda and Drea arrived at the house and seen that the front door was unlocked, and the garage was opened as well. They both knew there was foul play involved. Immediately they started to call Sasha's phone and any other phone numbers they could find of clients who might know her whereabouts. All numbers dialed were unsuccessful. Tajuanda looked up the last clients that were with Sasha and immediately seen they were fraud. She didn't know how she let this slip by her, being that she usually screened every client very carefully. She seen why they could have slipped by her but was mad she got caught slipping. Tajuanda made a mental promise that she would get Sasha back safely, no matter what because she felt at fault.

There was no trace of Sasha or her vehicle at the residence. Drea and Tajuanda split from each other, with the same mission on their minds, which was to find Sasha. They both knew in their hearts that Sasha was in great danger. Somehow Nick figured out a way to get Sasha alone and kidnapped her. They didn't know her whereabouts and knew it would be hard to find her. Tajuanda got on her phone and started to make phone calls. Drea was thinking about how she would tell everyone that Sasha was missing. The first person Drea called was Eric. Eric was in so much shock after the phone call that he dropped his phone and couldn't speak a word. Drea explained to him that she didn't know how she would go about telling Sasha's mother. Eric told her if she didn't feel comfortable, she should call Rebecca so she could tell Sasha's mother. Drea found that to be a good idea and called Rebecca. Rebecca was astounded. The news took her by so much of a surprise that she fell out and had to go to the hospital because she hit her head on a chair on her way to the ground.

After a while Rebecca called Drea back and informed her that she was at Sasha's mother's house and had told her what happened. She told Drea that she had an idea and wanted to meet her to talk. Rebecca also told Drea to bring Eric. After a while they met up at a park called Wes Montgomery. Drea chose the park because she knew Nick couldn't come nowhere near her neighborhood. Even after park hours they were still at the park like they were permitted to be there. Rebecca told them that she felt her boyfriend Nathan knew more about Nick than he had told her. She explained to them that there was no way Nathan could have run Nick's business the way he was without having communication with Nick. Rebecca was Sasha's best friend and she was going to do whatever she could do to make sure she was safe. So, the three of them talked and came up with a plan to try to get information out of Nathan.

Sasha was man handled off the plane. As soon as she could feel fresh air, all she could hear was Nick's voice. He took the blind fold off her face, looked her in the eyes and started laughing. He told her he still loved her and was proud of her, but she should have never crossed him. Nick told her that his intentions wasn't to kill her, but he wanted her to know he had the power to do whatever he wanted to do. He told her that he just wanted to talk to her to see if they could come to any type of understanding about the situation. Sasha stared at Nick and told him that he had to do what he had to do because she had nothing to say to him. That's when Nick told the guys to blind fold her again and take her to the warehouse. Sasha knew she was in Mexico but knew this trip would be nothing like it was when they were in Mexico for their honeymoon.

Sarah was still going through her thing with Tim. Tim had sent many people to try to kill her from jail. Sarah complained to the jail so much about what Tim was doing that they put Tim in solitary confinement where he couldn't talk to anyone. He sat in solitary confinement with rage in his heart, not knowing he would never have freedom again. While he was in there fighting the case on Sarah, prosecutors were building a whole other case on him that would lock him down for good as well.

Meanwhile, Rebecca, Drea and Eric were sitting at Waffle House waiting on Nathan to arrive. Rebecca called him and told him they needed to have a serious talk about Sasha. She told him that Drea and Eric would be in company so he wouldn't be surprised when he got there. Nathan didn't really want to go, but for his girlfriend he would do anything. Rebecca knew what

Nathan liked so she already had his Steak, Eggs, and Hash browns on the way when he got there.

Once Nathan sat at the table Rebecca got straight down to business. Nathan was surprised when she told him that Sasha was missing without a trace. Nathan had love for Sasha no matter what. After all he had grew up with her. They asked him if he had any clue about where Nick could be. Nathan told them that he knew for a fact Nick was hiding out in Mexico. He told them Nick never called him on the phone. The only way Nick communicated with him was through email. Nathan had no problem with taking them with him to show them the emails he received from Nick. Though they didn't know how his emails would help, they did want to see them just in case.

Drea called Tajuanda to see if anything could be done with the emails. Tajuanda told her that she could possibly track Nick from the emails, and she wanted to see them as well. After hanging up the phone with Drea, Tajuanda called her brother who worked for

Microsoft to ask him if he could hack into an email account. He told her it was easy to do and to just let him know when she was ready. Tajuanda had something up her sleeve for Nick. She was determined to take him down and show him that a Queen makes moves all around the world just like on a chess board. She knew Nick thought women were just good for sex, but she was about to show him that a woman could beat him even at his own game. For what he did to her sister she would never forgive him and shooting him dead would be too easy, she wanted him to suffer.

Sasha was in a dark room where she could hear nothing. She couldn't find it in her heart to be scared. Though she was still blind folded the darkness outside of the blind fold showed her that she was in the dark. She sat in silence for what seemed like forever. Then she started to hear voices speaking in Spanish. She spoke Spanish fluently, so she knew every word they were saying. She could hear a voice saying that he wanted to see who the lady was.

Someone turned on a light and Sasha could hear footsteps getting closer to her. A guy removed the blind fold from over her eyes. It was a short Mexican guy. He removed the blind fold and told his crew that he couldn't kill a woman so beautiful. Sasha still had on her work clothes. She was dressed in professional attire, but you could still see every curve on her body. Her beautiful face spoke for itself; she was drop dead gorgeous.

The Mexican guy asked her the weirdest question she had ever been asked or even heard before in life. He asked her if he could have the honor of kissing her feet. She had on open toed heels and she had some of the prettiest feet you could ever lay eyes on. Her thinking he was playing said yes, that's when he took her heels off and started sucking her toes. Sasha let out plenty of pleasurable moans, making him suck them more and more. She didn't know that this short Mexican guy had a thing for pretty feet and his thing for pretty feet could possibly save her life.

Toni was the name of the short Mexican. What Sasha didn't know was that he was the boss, the leader of the whole cartel. Nick brought Sasha to Mexico to kill her and bury her somewhere where she would never be thought of again. The thing was that when dealing with the cartel the boss had to approve of the situation for something like that to happen. Toni told his soldiers he couldn't approve of the killing of such a beautiful woman. He explained to them that he knows how to read eyes and that her eyes were innocent. After that he untied Sasha and told her they needed to have a talk. He told her he couldn't help himself when it came to tongue wrestling with her feet because they were the prettiest feet he had ever seen. Toni continuously apologized to her and told her he hoped she didn't feel violated. She let him know her feet had never felt so good in life and that he was a gentleman for asking first.

Nick was out taking care of business not knowing what was going on back at the warehouse.

Nick was just ready to get rid of Sasha and go back to Indianapolis to do away with Eric and Drea. He had a smile on his face from ear to ear because he loved the way his plans always came together, or so he thought. Nick knew Sasha worked for Tajuanda, but just didn't know if Tajuanda had mentioned anything to her. He knew Tajuanda would come for her, but in his thoughts, there would be nothing to find.

After talking to Toni for over an hour, he allowed Sasha to make a phone call. She told Toni about Nick raping her mother and getting her pregnant and all. He was very surprised about some of the things Sasha told him. He never took Nick for being that type of guy. He didn't just take Sasha's word for it though. Toni was an honest and fair man, so he made a few calls to verify the information Sasha had given him. After Toni verified all the information Sasha had given him, he let her know he was taking himself out of their situation. He gave her the green light to do whatever and told her that she didn't have to worry about none of the cartel troops at all.

What Nick didn't know is that Toni had love for women, especially beautiful ones. He was raised by his mother and she was the one who taught him everything. He became the leader of the cartel on his own because his mother always raised him right, but he took the wrong turn. He took the wrong turn partly because he wanted to have power to protect the women in his family. After seeing his mother get beat by numerous boyfriends and not being able to help, he made it his duty to rise to power and that's what he did. Toni was the most feared man in Mexico, with zero tolerance for men who battered women. Besides that, Nick made him a lot of money, but Nick drew too much heat and Toni didn't like being in the spotlight.

When Toni told Sasha to make her call, he informed her that Nick would know nothing about the call and told her to make a worthwhile call. Sasha called Eric. Eric was very shocked but happy at the same time to hear Sasha's voice. She told him where she was at and told him to tell Tajuanda and Drea that she needed them all there immediately. She let him know they could end Nick, but they needed to make a move quick. Eric's last words were, "say no more." Before he hung up the phone after writing down all the information he needed.

Toni tied Sasha back up, blind folded her, and put her in a cage to make it look like she was still about to die. Nick came back in the warehouse and smiled at the view of Sasha being in a cage; he loved the fact that she was about to die. He called out her name and asked her what she wanted her last meal to be before she died. Toni caged Sasha because he figured it would keep Nick from touching her. Toni was a very smart man. He knew that if it looked like she was already suffering Nick wouldn't be in a rush to kill her, because if he harmed her anymore Toni would have killed Nick himself. Toni didn't want to have to kill Nick himself, so he just tried to buy time to give Sasha enough time to do what she had to do.

Back in Indianapolis Drea was acting a fool. Drea was in rage and couldn't help but to resort to violence. She pulled up to Tonya's house and beat her down. She dragged her every which way and made her give her all the information about Nick she had. Tonya was on the ground begging Drea to stop beating her. Then Drea's other friend Chanda got out the car with a cup of salt. She walked up to Tonya and started to pour the salt in her mouth. That's when Tonya gave up and gave them the phone number Nick had been calling from. After that Drea kicked Tonya one more time in the face and they left Tonya's house.

As soon as Drea pulled off she called Eric on the phone. Eric told her that he had been trying to call her but didn't receive an answer. He told her Sasha called him and that Tajuanda was getting their flights booked as he spoke. Drea was very happy to hear the news. She told him about what she had just done. Eric told her not to call the number and to go back and tie Tonya up before she could get back in touch with Nick. Drea made a U-turn and went right back to Tonya's house. Drea walked right up to Tonya's door and kicked it in, her and Chanda walked straight in and got down to business. They tied Tonya up and started drinking from Tonya's personal bar in her house. Tonya wasn't worried about being tied up because she knew her male friend would be there before long. To her surprise though Drea told Chanda to go pull her car in the garage so they could take Tonya with them. Drea was no rookie to the game and knew someone would be there to check on Tonya some time. She didn't want any slip ups so she figured she would just take Tonya with them.

CHAPTER 13

On the other note, Nick's wife in California had enough of him. Everything he had in her name she took ownership over. She took all the cash he had in their house, along with their children, and ran off to a place she never thought Nick could find her. She put everything up for sale, even the business that Nick was about to put on the stock market. Nick had worn out his welcome with her and she was tired of being married to a man she never seen. Since she helped him build most of his businesses, she felt it was only right that she kept them.

Nathan was also washing his hands of Nick. Nathan was never a money hungry guy, but now he felt like he was letting money get to his head. It was like Nick had him trained ever since the trip they took to Florida. Being that Nathan came from nothing, of course the money was flattering, but he still had morals. He knew Nick and Sasha were going through things but didn't know the extreme. As a good man, he couldn't help a man that did his friend wrong.

Nathan didn't know that his life was just about to begin. Nick's wife had seen what he did for the company through her database and wanted him on her team when she was to take full ownership over the business. Nathan was an honest guy overall and she could tell that by the dedication he showed to his work. Even the deals he completed where he could have held something back, he didn't, and Kim seen that. She planned on selling everything co owned with Nick and doing her own thing and when she did, she planned on Nathan being the first person she hired.

The city of Indianapolis was still in an uproar. People having shoot outs over drug territory, teenagers killing teenagers, and kids having kids. The east side of Indianapolis was like Afghanistan. It was either kill or be killed. While the west side was bad too, there was still more unity. So many robberies went down all around the city that you would have thought robbery was legal, being that it was so common.

Drea, Tajuanda and Eric's plane landed in Midland, Texas, where a chauffeur was waiting on them to take them into El Paso, Texas. As soon as they arrived in El Paso, they went to eat at What A Burger and talked about the plan they formulated. After eating they went to meet up with members of a Mexican cartel that Tajuanda knew. They crossed into Mexico through an underground tunnel riding four wheelers with a mass load of firearms and ammunition. Tajuanda also brought a nice stash of cash to be generous to the cartel for their help. They found it to be a better idea to go into Mexico undetected, so they wouldn't have to cross the border and it be known they were there. It was time for business, and they didn't want anything to stop their mission.

It had been weeks since Nick's wife Kim had heard from him. She knew he was up to no good by the way he stayed away from home with no contact. Then after seeing him on FBI's most wanted, she knew she did the right thing by fleeing from him. Even after taking everything and fleeing from him she still didn't have closure. She was just curious about a few things and wanted answers to the many questions she had in her mind. What Nick didn't know is that he left too many trails behind that Kim could pick up on and find out what she needed to know. Kim figured Nick knew Nathan and since she did want Nathan to work for her, she figured she would ask Nathan some questions.

It was a chilly, but not cold winter day when Kim touched down in Indianapolis, Indiana. She came off the flight in a pink and gray Gucci sweat suit and Jordan's on to match. Though she usually wore business attire she still had a fetish for Jordan's and nice sweat suits. She went to Avis to rent a car and was on her way to meet Nathan. Not knowing what she would find out, she just took her time to get to her Indianapolis Enterprise. She had been to Indianapolis a few times before, so she knew her way to Keystone at the Crossings.

Kim came into the office with many people looking at her like she was a stranger. Many men looked at her with lust, as her butt bounced from left to right and the way her titties bounced up and down in her zip up sweatshirt. You couldn't deny or overlook the beauty of her face and any man whether married or not could only admire the shape of her perfect body. She was hated on by many women, but she wasn't conceited or arrogant at all. Kim wanted to be loved and be one man's only woman like any other woman wanted. Many of the women who hated on her only hated because they knew she could take their man if she wanted to, but Kim wasn't like that at all. Kim was just Kim and she was cool as hell.

Kim approached the receptionist and asked for Nathan. When they asked who, she was, she told them Kim Terry. No one knew Nick by John Terry, so the last name didn't ring a bell to the receptionist, so she treated Kim like a customer and not part owner of the enterprise that employed her. Kim took it in and was just trying to do what she came to do, which was to find out what Nick was up to in Indianapolis. Once she was in Nathan's office she got straight down to business. Nathan told her he didn't want to talk in his office, so they decided to go to Benihana's, which was right down the street.

While Nick was sitting with his crew getting the last details together on killing Sasha and making her body disappear, Tajuanda, Drea and Eric were meeting with Toni. What laid ahead was going to be a shock to Nick, but when snakes made snake moves an even bigger snake always laid in the cut ready to bite. Nick had his mind made up that anyone who crossed him would die and he lived by that code his whole life. Even when he walked on the right side of life, he still had his mind made up to kill all his enemies.

Nick really could have been a great legit businessman. After getting released from prison he was doing the right thing for a while, but just got bored with it. He had money put up from before he went to prison and after getting possession of the money again, he invested the money into his club in Texas. Nick may have put every bit of three-hundred thousand into that club, but through his negotiations and keen eye for business he turned the initial investment into over two million dollars in less than two years. Nick was very smart when it came to business, but if business didn't come with dodging police, it really wasn't interesting to Nick. He made it rich the legit way and still wanted to be in the streets, only because Nick wanted to make dummies out of the police.

As Kim and Nathan sat watching the chef cook their Hibachi Chicken Rice, with extra garlic butter and Yum Yum sauce, they talked about Nick. Nathan didn't want to say much, but felt it was necessary considering the circumstances behind his friend Sasha. He told Kim about Sasha being Nicks wife, which caught Kim by surprise considering she never knew him as Nick

Burton. He told her about Nick kidnapping Sasha, her mother, and his own son. After he told her about Nick impregnating Sasha's mother from raping her, Kim got so disgusted that she had to leave. Nathan gave the cashier a hundred-dollar bill on the way out of the restaurant and told her to keep the change for meals they never ate.

After getting to her rental car, Kim broke out in tears and told Nathan she needed to talk to Sasha's mother immediately. Nathan hesitated, but gave in to call Tammy and ask if it would be okay to bring Kim by the house. After a lot of persuading from Nathan, Tammy agreed to meet Kim under the agreement that they meet at a public place.

While Kim talked to Tammy, they both were in tears. They both hugged each other and tried to keep their composure. By the end of the conversation, Kim vowed that she would find out where Nick was at with Sasha and wouldn't leave Indianapolis until Sasha was back home. Kim told Tammy information Nick would have never known she knew. She told her about children Nick had that no one knew he had. Kim told her about the horrible childhood Nick had that resulted in him killing his own brother. She even told her about the reason why Nick's oldest daughter would have nothing to do with Nick.

Nick's parents were very abusive to him as a child. The abuse lead to him tying them up to their bed one night. Afterwards he burned the house down with them left inside to burn alive. After Nick's oldest daughter's mother died, he ran off with her best friend and his daughter would never forgive him for that neither. Nicks real family feared him but felt sorry for him because they felt his parents made him the way he was. No one really knew the story behind Nick, but the ones who did knew to never tell. The only reason Kim knew so much information is because he was away from home so much that she had time to dig in deep on him. Plus, she had access to files that average citizens didn't have access to.

Kim left from meeting with Tammy and Nathan and headed to the Hilton Hotel to make some connections and find out Nick's whereabouts. Tammy gave her Rebecca's phone number so she could call her to get more information about Sasha's kidnapping. Kim called her uncle and had him run a trace and GPS on every phone number she knew Nick possessed. Three of the GPS alerts hit in Mexico, so that's where she was sending the police to. She hated Nick after the news she heard and made a mental promise that he would never see their children again.

Nick sat at the table with his soldiers eating fruit off a fruit tray, he soaked all the fruit in Patron Tequila before putting it back on the tray. As he ate the fruit, he was making jokes about how he was going to kill Sasha. Nick had his mind set on making Sasha out of an example. Sasha wasn't the only one he planned on killing neither. He also wanted Drea and Eric to suffer even more. He cemented his plan, gave his soldiers the nod, and headed to the warehouse to finish out his plan.

His soldiers knew what was about to happen to him, but never said a word. Nick's crew knew Toni would have them and their families killed if they warned Nick about anything. They had the same fear for Nick at first, but always knew Toni was their real boss and could knock them out the box quicker than Nick could ever imagine. They talked amongst each other all the time about how cruel Nick was, but they went along with him because it was their job.

Nick and his soldiers walked into the dark warehouse. Nick came in saying the words, "bitch daddy's home and brought you a tricky treat."

After that he broke out laughing and so did his soldiers. The soldiers only laughed because they knew Nick's plan was about to backfire in his face. Nick going down brought a relief to them because they had never worked for such a cruel boss. Nick had a bathtub he was going to lay Sasha in full of wet cement and planned to let it harden around her body while she was still alive. He was about to make her die a miserable death. Nick then told his soldier to turn on the lights.

Right when he told him to turn on the lights, he heard a voice that sounded like Tajuanda's say, "I believe I can help you with that."

That's when the lights came on and he seen the faces of Sasha, Drea, Eric and Tajuanda. He looked at Sasha and laughed asking her if she was dressing up for Halloween. Sasha was dressed in an all pink cat woman suit with a platinum cat woman mask on. Her body looked stunning in this body suit, as you could see her beautifully sculpted body.

"You mother fuckers really done fucked up now, it's even better now because I don't have to travel to the city to kill the rest of you dummies. And Sasha that ass is looking fat in that cat suit, I'm a fuck you one last time after I kill you bitch. Can't believe you dumb bitches would come to my territory thinking you could do something to me. And Eric you know I owe you a bullet to the head for old times' sake, you pussy," said Nick as he continued to laugh.

As Nick continued to laugh Toni came through the door to order Nick's soldiers out of the room. Before Toni told Nick's soldiers to leave the room Nick said, "yeah you dumb bitches really about to die now. Stupid bitches than just fucked with the wrong one and Eric I want a one on one fight with you before I kill you thinking you captain save a hoe or something."

Nick's whole facial expression changed after Toni ordered his soldiers to leave the room. He still stood strong cussing them out and calling them every disrespectful name that came to mind. It all changed when Eric hit him in the mouth knocking him to the ground and Sasha put her open toed stiletto covered foot in his neck. Drea continuously stomped Nick as he laid on the ground. That was the game changer for Nick right there. He was wondering why the fuck Toni and all his soldiers just left him like that.

While this was going on Kim was on the phone alerting the FBI that she knew the whereabouts of her so-called husband John Terry. The authorities told her they couldn't just walk into Mexico to take him, so they had to get permission from Mexico's authorities to cross the border. Kim didn't know about Tajuanda, Eric, and Drea being there, so she told them to hurry because he had a hostage from America. That's when the FBI director got on the phone calling who he needed to call, so the FBI could cross the border. Kim just kept her fingers crossed that the police would get to Mexico in time to save Sasha.

Sasha stared Nick straight in the eyes as she stood over him with her foot in his neck. Eric also stared at him with a fully loaded 500 magnum pointed at his head. Sasha still looked sexy in her cat suit even with the holstered Glock 17 on her waist. Tajuanda had some words she wanted to say to him before they killed him. She told him that she told him he would pay for throwing her sister in front of the bullet that was meant to kill him. Sasha and Eric looked at Tajuanda in amazement, being that they never knew Tajuanda knew who Nick was. Sasha now understood why Tajuanda helped her so much. Sasha now felt that Tajuanda helped her because she knew how it felt to be hurt by Nick too. At this point Sasha didn't care what was going on she just knew she loved Tajuanda with all her heart.

Tajuanda then looked at Sasha and told her that she knew everything Nick had done to her and that's why she wanted to help her. She told her that she knew Nick would come to kill her and wanted her fully prepared for him when he came. Though she never knew Nick would be smart enough to pull off a kidnapping the way he kidnapped Sasha. She told Sasha that her worrying days were over as they both shed a tear and hugged. Nick looked from them to the door thinking Toni and his soldiers would come in, but to his surprise they didn't.

As soon as Sasha released her foot from Nick's neck, he grabbed his neck and caught his breath. After a few more minutes of watching Tajuanda talk to Sasha, Nick tried to make a run for the door. He was cut short when Eric hit him in the head with his gun. After that Sasha shot him in the back and he hit the ground. Tajuanda then opened the side door to the warehouse and let four natural bred Kita dogs in that were trained to kill, to finish Nick off.

As they turned to walk out the door Tajuanda looked back at Nick and said, "I told you I'd have the last laugh you dirty grimy son of a bitch."

Sasha and Eric just looked at Nick and walked away, but Drea spit on him and said, "this is for my cousin you killed bitch."

After that they walked out the door and locked it behind them, as the dogs started the tear into Nick's flesh. The crew walked up to a parked Jeep Wrangler, as Tajuanda told them how proud she was of them. Tajuanda told them she had been waiting to kill Nick for several years. As they left, she told them the story of why she wanted to kill Nick. She told them how much she suffered each day on earth without her sister. They all felt sorry and tried to console her, but Tajuanda told them that she now had the closure she needed.

No one was left in the warehouse, but Nick and the vicious dogs. After Toni told Nick's soldiers to leave the warehouse, he took them to eat Tacos and drink. As Toni ate his tacos all he could think about was Sasha, he felt she was innocent and beautiful. He thought to himself that he would have given her the world if she was his, but she let a punk like Nick take advantage of her. Toni loved the way her toes felt in his mouth and would never forget the taste. He thought to himself as he giggled, "I guess that's the influence a beautiful woman can have on a boss." Toni had broken every code in his cartel to save Sasha and didn't think twice about doing it. His cartel brothers were supposed to come before his blood family, no matter if they were right or wrong. That was an oath each member vowed to before becoming a member. Toni had now broken the code he made and was proud of it.

Nick hollered and hollered as the Kita's tore into his flesh, then out of nowhere the door was being kicked in. FBI agents swarmed the building shooting every dog that bit into Nick. Nick was seconds from having his life taken away from him, but to his surprise the FBI saved his life. They saved his life in the flesh because they planned to put him in prison for the rest of his natural life. They had to lifeline him to a hospital in Mexico and put him into immediate surgery. He had a gunshot wound to the back and plenty of bites from the dogs to go with it, along with a swollen face from being hit with the gun by Eric. Nick literally had less than a minute left of living before the dogs would have taken his life.

CHAPTER 14

Tajuanda and the crew decided to take a trip to Cancun before going back to Indianapolis. Though Sasha did want to be back with her son as soon as possible. She knew a trip to the beach would clear her mind and put her mind state in a settled mode before returning home. After all she had been held captive for over a week and experienced the worst feeling she ever felt in life. Not knowing what would happen to her had her ready to faint while she was in that warehouse. Kicking up some sand sounded very peaceful to Sasha and that's what her and three of her favorites were about to do.

Sasha couldn't stop crying after all the violence was over. She didn't cry because she killed two people and shot two people, which is something she never thought she would have to do in life. She cried because she couldn't believe Tajuanda, Drea, and Eric risked their own lives to come to Mexico and save her. She couldn't thank them enough. She thanked them so much that they started thanking her also, to stop her from thanking them. In her mind, she knew they were the true meaning of friends. She knew Rebecca would do the same, but they were new to her and to go out on such a limb for her so soon only made her feel even more special. So, for the moment Sasha figured she would leave all her painful memories in Indianapolis and enjoy her mini vacation in Mexico.

After going shopping for clothes, Sasha and the rest of the crew headed to the resort. The three ladies shared a room and since Eric was the only male, he had a room of his own. Tajuanda paid for everything. Tajuanda told Drea and Eric that once they returned to Indianapolis, she would make them real estate agents for her company also. She said she never in all her years of living seen a group of people show so much love to one another. She told them that their loyalty for each other made them a part of her company, not what they knew about real estate. That news had Drea and Eric lost for words, as they both needed more money to invest into their dreams. She also told Eric he was making history with being the first man to join, Straight Thang Realty.

Drea, Tajuanda, and Eric all headed for the beach, while Sasha stayed in the hotel room to clear some things off her mind. She ordered a pizza, a pitcher of Cherry Coke, and a fruit tray with fruit dip from room service. They said it would be about thirty minutes, so she figured she would take a shower while she waited on her food. She took a hot steamy shower that she wanted to last forever. She thought about all that happened in her life and was just happy that the man who caused all her pain was dead. The hotel room she was in brought back memories of Nick. She remembered being on her honeymoon in the same hotel making love to Nick all over the place.

Back in Indianapolis, Rebecca was sitting with Kim, Tammy and Nathan. Kim told them that the FBI had Nick in custody, which made them all smile. Then the news came that there was no trace of Sasha and they all went into a frenzy. That's when an email came to Sasha's mother from Sasha, telling her that she was okay and would be back to Indianapolis in a couple days. This news brought her mother relief right in the nick of time. Everyone else was happy when she told them Sasha was okay as well. They hugged Kim and didn't want to let her go. Kim then told them that their pain along with her pain was over with.

Kim or none of the rest of them knew what transpired in Mexico, but Kim did get the news that Nick was life lined to a hospital in critical condition. She told the other three about the news of his condition and no one seemed to care. Kim looked at Tammy and told her how sorry she was for what happened to her and her family in the hands of Nick. Tammy was due to have her baby by Nick in a matter of weeks and as the day came closer, she stressed more and more. Though now she did have some closure knowing that Nick was behind bars and would probably be there for life. She knew she would never have full closure because she was still about to have a baby by the monster.

While all this was going on, Sarah and Valarie were having a simple lunch at Subway on the east side of Indianapolis. Neither of them knew what was going on with Sasha or Eric, but they did worry about them. Sarah told Valarie that Tim had gotten ahold of a cellular phone in jail and had been in contact with her. Sarah told her that she didn't want to see Tim behind bars and was contemplating giving him another chance. Sarah also informed her that Tim's sister was going to meet her at the Subway they were eating at to discuss Tim's criminal case.

Valarie told Sarah to stay far away from Tim and any of his family or associate's because she knew how dangerous Tim could be. Sarah had her mind made up that Tim had changed, and she wanted to give him another chance. She had never heard Tim cry before and after hearing him cry her heart opened for him again. Sarah told Valarie that she wasn't going to be a part of Eric's program anymore. Valarie didn't agree with Sarah's decision, but knew she couldn't do anything but deal with it. She knew Sarah was grown and made her own decisions in life. She just wondered what was going to happen with Sarah and her move to Arizona.

Eric's phone had been going to voicemail, but when Valarie tried to call him again it finally rang. She told him about the conversation she had with Sarah and after that all you heard was silence on the phone. Eric had worked very hard to get all the women in his program mentally strong, so to hear of news like that he was astounded. He informed Valarie that he would be back to Indianapolis within the next 48 hours. He also told her that he would try to call Sarah to talk some sense into her, though when he did call, he seen that Sarah blocked his number. Eric knew that news would make Sasha very sad being that she had shot Tim trying to protect Sarah.

Sasha got out the shower and put on her night clothes. She said in her mind that she was just going to eat and lounge around watching television until she fell asleep. Once her food came, she turned on the television and ate as she watched the local news. She ate the pizza thinking about when Nick ordered pizza for her on their honeymoon while shaking her head. She couldn't believe how things went from being so sweet to being so sour with him. She knew she couldn't take anything back, so she just focused her mind on other things.

Tajuanda, Drea, and Eric were out on the beach enjoying themselves. Drea and Tajuanda were the hot topic of the beach. They had drunk more than five shots each and didn't have to pay for any of them. With butt's so big, no stomach, and big titties, men couldn't keep their eyes off them and was doing anything to be in their presence. Neither of them was rude to the men who tried to holler at them, but they did let them know that they weren't interested. Eric was doing his own thing enjoying the views of the water and conversating with many beautiful ladies.

Sasha woke up after a brief nap to breaking news on the news station. She recognized the warehouse on the news because it was the one, she just left from. To her surprise though, Nick was still alive. She did see that the FBI had taken him into custody but wondered how he survived such a vicious attack. This was not news Sasha wanted to see or hear. She knew Nick was smart and could probably figure his way out of a criminal case, though she did doubt it because his charges were so severe. The reporter took over two minutes to read off all of Nick's criminal charges. They said he would be in Mexico until after his surgeries were finished and then he would be extradited back to Indianapolis. He faced charges in Indianapolis and eighteen other states, and they were still filing charges.

Sasha slipped on a sun dress, said forget underwear, and some sandals then headed to the beach to tell the rest of the crew what was going on with Nick.

Sasha finally found the crew on the beach, the three of them were relaxing and enjoying themselves. They all looked at her face and knew something was wrong with her. When they asked, she told them that Nick didn't die, and that Federal agents had him in custody. They asked how she knew, and she told them it was breaking news in Mexico. Though none of them knew it was breaking news in Indianapolis as well. When she told them they all wondered how the authorities were brought into the equation period. They all wanted him dead instead of in prison, considering they all knew of guilty people getting off on cases every day. Sasha really dreaded him going to jail because she knew one way or another, she would have to testify on him. Sasha never wanted to lay eyes on Nick again. For some reason now, she felt like Nick would never be out of her life. Then she still had to deal with the fact that her mother would be having a baby by him soon. Sasha's thoughts were now all over the place.

Tajuanda looked at Sasha and said, "sweetie, don't worry, Nick will never see another day of freedom again. They will give that son of a bitch multiple life sentences, now enjoy this beach woman." Then she hugged Sasha as Sasha took a seat on the beach with them and ordered a much-needed Pina Colada.

They then agreed that they would cut their mini vacation short and head back to Indianapolis by morning. None of them were upset about leaving before they originally planned, because they all had other business to take care of. They all told Sasha to cheer up and enjoy the beach for the night, which is what she did. Sasha wasn't a drinker, but she dug in on a bottle of Don Julio mixed with pineapple juice after her Pina Colada. Sasha got to feeling tipsy and got up dancing to almost every song, it was surely a night to remember. The four of them partied like they didn't have a care in the world. Sasha's naked body would show every time the wind blew her dress up, but she didn't care. Eric would laugh and turn his head, but other men waited for the wind to blow so they could see her body again.

Sasha wasn't the only one surprised when she seen the news that Nick wasn't dead. Toni seen the news and immediately got mad. He didn't know how it happened, but he was going to finish it off. Toni had every connection you could have in Mexico. He just had to figure out a way to get someone in the hospital to kill Nick without being caught by the federal agents. Toni didn't want to risk the chance of Nick being able to tell on his whole organization, so he wanted him dead. Nick knew too much information for Toni to let him walk free. Toni went to his drawing board and attempted to formulate a plan to kill Nick.

Valarie was finishing up the last of her chores around her house. Things were back in line for her and she was proud of herself for once in life. Her new salon was looking to generate over one hundred thousand dollars that year and she was still making room for the many other stylist who wanted to rent booth space. She had the set up for a spa to be put in the back of her salon. In no way was she thinking small and this time she was determined to never let a man take anything else from her again. After reading, "Women Stop Falling 4 No Good Men," and listening to Eric speak every week, she felt she had all the motivation she needed to stand strong alone until her Mr. Right came along. The news that laid ahead of her would totally catch her off guard though.

Tammy was sitting there watching her grandson, listening to Brian McKnight, "One last cry." She had her husband on her mind heavy. It was like her world had shattered on her, though no one could tell. Kim was very generous to her and promised her she would do whatever she could for her. After hearing the news of what Nick did to Sasha and her family, Kim told Tammy that forty-nine percent of the Indianapolis enterprise belonged to them once she took full ownership. Plus, Kim said she was relocating to Indianapolis. Tammy wondered why Kim was doing so much, but she just didn't know that Kim had her own problems back in Cali and just wanted to be around good people.

Out of nowhere Tammy started to feel stomach pain. She ran to the restroom and blood came from her vagina like a faucet. She called Rebecca and told her to get there immediately and called the ambulance as well. Rebecca got there before the ambulance and took Sasha's son with her before Tammy went to the hospital. After hours of being in the hospital room on medication, the doctor came in the room and told Tammy that the baby had lost her heartbeat. Tammy cried because she was just that type of person. In a way, she figured it would save the baby much pain that may have come her way in the future though.

Nick laid in his hospital bed under the influence of so much medication that he couldn't feel anything. All he heard was the words of the doctor, he was wishing he was just living in a dream. He was handcuffed with over a dozen armed federal agents around him. The doctor told him that he was paralyzed from his neck down to his feet. He couldn't believe the words he just heard. It was then that he started to go back and picture all the wrong he had done to everyone. The shot that Sasha gave him to his back paralyzed him for life. Though he was in the worst position he had been in his whole life, he still managed to have hateful thoughts towards Sasha. Even under the influence of many different medications his eagerness to kill Sasha was still there, especially after he found out he was paralyzed.

Live breaking news was broadcasting in Indianapolis. Valarie looked at the scenery behind the Fox 59 newscaster and the scenery looked very familiar. A body had been found in the trunk of a car. When Valarie saw the 2004 Cadillac STS, she fell to the floor. She knew it was Sarah's car. The newscaster said that Sarah had been taken away from the Subway at 10th and Arlington Avenue and brought back lifeless to be placed in the trunk of her car. A witness walking to the drugstore saw the body being put in the trunk and ran to the payphone to call the police. Though the suspects did get away, there was a clear description of the getaway vehicle including the license plate number. The newscaster said the detectives were investigating why the suspects would take her away and then bring her back. They were wrecking their brains trying to figure out where the real murder scene was at.

So much had happened over the past year that it was almost breaking everyone in Sasha's circle. The fact that they were all genuinely good people made things even worst for them because they didn't want to be violent. Valarie thought about what Eric said one day in his speech. Eric's words were, "the devil doesn't come to make his presence known, instead he comes to make you feel his presence." Those words kept on playing in Valarie's mind as she cried over the loss of her dear friend. She had so many wonderful memories with her, it just didn't seem real that Sarah was gone. Valarie made up in her mind then that any man who was no good had to be sent by the devil. She felt that way because every woman in Eric's group sessions still felt the pain of the no-good man they left. Her goal now was to stay far away from no-good men.

Tajuanda, Sasha, Drea, and Eric sat in the first-class section of their flight. Sasha's mind was now clearer than it had ever been over the past year and a half of dealing with Nick. She felt good that the pain was finally over with, she also smiled at the thought that she could finally go back to her normal life. She knew the memories would still be there, but she knew that once she hugged her baby boy the feeling of joy would be right back in her heart. As Xscape's song "Understanding," played in her headphones, she laid back in her seat and closed her eyes. She thought to herself, "If only I'd have read Eric's book before I started dealing with Nick."

CHAPTER 15

Drea was driving Sasha to her personal vehicle after the flight. There really wasn't many words exchanged between her and Drea, but Drea did tell her how proud she was of her for standing strong. Drea had to call Chanda to tell her that she could let Tonya go. Sasha looked at her as she talked on the phone with a confused look on her face. Drea then told her what she did before going to Mexico. Sasha looked at her and smiled. Sasha knew since day one, Drea always had her back. Sasha told her that she was going to do something real nice for her when everything was all said and done. That's when Drea told her that she didn't owe her anything and to just keep being herself.

Sasha walked into her mother's house and seen her mother on the couch looking very sad. She told her to not look sad no more and asked if she was okay. That didn't change the expression on her mother's face, but she got up and hugged Sasha real tight. While hugging her she told Sasha that the baby had died. Sasha looked at her but didn't know what to say. Then her mother told her to call Valarie as soon as possible. Sasha told her mother she would call Valarie after she seen her son. As soon as she found her son in his room, she woke him up while picking him up and kissing him all over his face.

Sasha let her son go back to sleep before she picked up her phone to call Valarie, but before she could dial the number Eric was calling her. Sasha could hear his tears through the phone as he told her the news about Sarah. Sasha broke down right after hearing the dreadful words. Sarah was such a sweet woman to Sasha, ever since they had met each other they clicked to one another. Sasha told Eric she was on her way to wherever he was at but told him she needed to get off the phone so she could call Valarie first.

Sasha was only a twenty-three-year-old woman. After all she had been through, her pain made her a forty-year-old woman in the soul. Jamal was walking around the house getting into everything and he was her pride and joy. The words that kept Sasha in high spirits were the words her father once spoke to her while she was going through her breakup with Ronald. Her father told her, "For every lesson you go through in life, there are two blessings waiting after you outlast that lesson, don't give up Sasha." She thought about those words and put her game face back on. She knew what she had to do.

After meeting with Eric and Valarie, Sasha headed back to her mother's house. When she got in the house, she was greeted by a beautiful white woman she had never seen before. Kim introduced herself to Sasha and told her the reason she came from California to Indianapolis. Sasha looked at Kim like she was a ghost when she mentioned she was Nick's wife and had three children by him. Sasha had been through so much and didn't know what was going on. She told Kim to leave her mother's house thinking it was another one of Nick's set ups. After Kim told her about all the trouble, she went through to find her in Mexico, Sasha changed her mind. Kim went on to tell her that she was the one who alerted the FBI and told them where Nick had her held captive at. Sasha couldn't help but to give her a hug after that.

Kim invited Sasha to go to Starbucks with her to have some coffee and talk about some things. Sasha went with her and they sat talking for over an hour. After the talk, they both were seeing eye to eye and agreed that Jamal needed to know his siblings. Neither of them knew the whereabouts of all Nick's other children but did know they existed. They figured they would start trying to find them on another day. Both ladies knew they had enough on their plates for the time being.

The next day, everyone met up at Sasha's apartment to eat, drink, and talk about some things. The normal crew was there including Kim, Nathan, and Rebecca. Tajuanda thanked Kim for putting in the effort she had put in to bring Sasha home safe. When Sasha first told Tajuanda about Kim, Tajuanda didn't get a good feeling about her. After a while she felt Kim did more than most would have. Tajuanda made sure Kim knew that she was a hero in her eyes. Then Kim went to shake hands with Eric, and they couldn't keep their eyes off each other.

Kim and Eric sat on the couch getting to know each other, while everyone else sat at the table playing cards, laughing, and talking. By the end of the night Kim and Eric had a day and time to go out on their first date. Kim made sure Eric knew that she would be divorced from Nick within a two-week time period. She also told him about her three children and her plans to make their new home in Indianapolis. Eric's mind was all over the place, but one thing that never changed is the fact that he knew he wanted to be with Kim. He didn't know how those feelings came about so fast, but he was digging her physically and mentally.

The coroner released Sarah's body after two weeks to the funeral home. They said she died from being hit in the head with a blunt object. Sarah had been so badly beaten that there was no way she could have an open casket. They found DNA under her nails and the DA's office found a positive match for the DNA. Sarah did fight for her life, but she couldn't fight her killer or killers off her completely. No one was ready to hear this news. Her family did let Sasha, Eric, and Valarie help them make her funeral arrangements. Her family was so devastated that they didn't know where to start at arranging her funeral.

Tim sat in jail thinking he was going to get his charges dropped now that Sarah was dead. To his surprise the police had too much evidence linking him to the killer. And even more to his surprise they had someone in custody for questioning. The man whose car was used to take Sarah back to the Subway was in custody. He was a man who really didn't know anything, but he did know enough for the detectives to build a case. He told them who he let borrow his car. The detectives were then headed over to Tim's cell in solitary confinement to question him. After questioning him, they read him his rights and charged him with conspiracy to commit murder. That charge along with all his other charges would send Tim to prison for life, without ever having the possibility of parole.

The police located the man who used the guy's car and it surprised them that the guy started snitching before he even made it back to police headquarters. He told them Tim paid him and threatened him into killing Sarah. He told how Tim was able to get a cellular phone in jail and everything. He even told about other unsolved murders Tim had committed in the past as well. Though Tim didn't have power like Nick, he was still a dangerous and connected man while on the streets. The man told police that Sasha was next on Tim's murdering list too.

Toni's plan to assassinate Nick wasn't successful. Though he made over four attempts, his hit team couldn't get around the federal agents. There was so much security around Nick that you would have thought he was the most wanted man ever. After getting back to Indianapolis, Nick was put in protective custody. Guards put him there for his own safety, but also because they wanted to monitor everything he did. What they didn't know is that Nick no longer had the power he once had. He now only had a few people in the Indianapolis area who would ride for him. The police knew he was paralyzed, but also knew that if he could talk, he was still a dangerous man.

Nick sat in Marion County Jail not knowing what was going on in the streets. He tried to call Kim several times, but never received an answer. He didn't know that she didn't want anything else to do with him. He had plans of paying the best lawyer in Indianapolis to represent him, but just didn't know that he had no money left. All his businesses were gone now. Kim made sure she took his name off everything they once co owned. It wasn't hard for her to do because he used a fake name anyway.

As the federal Marshall's wheeled Nick into the federal courtroom in downtown Indianapolis, he investigated the crowd. In the crowd amongst many others there was Sasha, Tammy, Tajuanda, Drea, Eric, Kim, Valarie, Kim's brother and Drea's cousin Damo. Nick double looked when he seen Eric with his arm around Kim, then shouted, "Bitch ass nigga," and started punching in the air since he couldn't walk. It seemed like if he could have walked, he would have been in the crowd swinging. Eric kissed Kim on the lips then smiled at Nick and winked after his outburst. A federal Marshall told Nick if he had another outburst, he wouldn't see the judge for six months. Nick couldn't believe what he was seeing. The only thing he asked himself was how it all came about. By this time, he knew that Kim had taken everything from him, that made him even more pissed. Then as he looked at Eric more, he seen that Eric had on one of his suits. It was a brand-new suit that Nick had never worn. Nick knew it was his because he had it made by a special Tailor, so he knew no one else in the world had one like it.

The judge told Nick in arraignment that the United States of Southern Indiana was charging him with the RICO Act. Then informed him that it carried a mandatory life sentence in Federal Prison. Nick then looked to the crowd at Sasha as she winked at him and stuck her tongue out seductively. Drea got up to make her presence be known and looked at him with duck lips smiling. Nick now wished he had of just died back in Mexico. He thought he could beat his charges because that's what type of person he was, but after he seen the crowd, he knew that dream was over for him. With so many witnesses there was no way he was going to walk free.

There was a delay at the elevator, so Nick could see everyone exit the court room. Kim, Sasha and everyone else walked out like they were all one big happy family. Nick didn't see Nathan, so he thought he would hit him up, but he would soon find out that Nathan now worked for Kim. Not only that but now the enterprise was partly owned by Sasha and her mother as well. All walls were closed in on Nick.

Kim, Sasha, and Tammy changed the whole way the enterprise operated. They also gave Nathan the power to change anything he wanted in the enterprise, without having to consult with them. After all, it was Nathan who took the enterprise to the next level as soon as he came on board. Everyone felt it would only be right to let Nathan have some real power now. Nathan was no longer a puppet for Nick.

Sarah's funeral was the saddest funeral Sasha had ever attended. She couldn't believe a woman had lost her life by the hands of a no-good man. Sarah had a bright future ahead of her. They were all sad when Sarah told them she was moving to Arizona. Now they only wished she had of moved to Arizona so they could at least talk to her and visit her. Sarah's casket sat there closed as everyone observed her pictures in remembrance of her. Sasha couldn't even stay the whole funeral, because she couldn't hold back her tears.

Sasha ended up getting everything back that Nick had bought for her, including all the vehicles he had bought her as wedding gifts. Nick was being served a series of papers, from his divorces to the confiscation papers of everything he thought he still owned. Sasha donated everything she was able to get back from Nick, except the vehicles. Staff at the Julian Center for Women in Indianapolis was very happy to receive the donations from Sasha.

AFTERWORD

Nick's trial lasted over three weeks, he was convicted of the RICO Act and sentenced to life in prison. Though he still had hope he would overturn his sentence in an appeal. As he was wheeled around the prison yard of USP McCreary which was a high security federal prison, he thought about the fact that he was once a rich man, but now he had nothing. He was still trying to figure out a way to kill Sasha, Kim, Tajuanda, Drea and Eric. His plans were always cut short because he had no connections to the outside world. After Nick was sentenced to life in prison, most of the other judicial systems dropped their charges against him. Most knew he would never see the day of light again, but others kept their charges against him just in case he did get an appeal.

Nick heard many stories about what was going on in the streets, and the fact that Kim was now married to Eric really made him upset. Eric was seen with his kids all the time and it seemed that they were living a happy life. Nick would get occasional pictures of his kids, but never knew where they came from. Even after everything Nick was going through, he still didn't regret anything he did to anyone. He survived in prison off his job in the law library, which only paid him eighty dollars a month. Nick knew law very well after spending fifteen years of his life in prison before his life sentence.

Drea was living out her dreams. She had her nail salon, worked in real estate with Tajuanda and had other business ventures going on with Sasha. She had money put up for her son to attend college without a student loan. She had a boyfriend but told him they would never live together unless they were married. Drea had been through her own pain in life and learned many valuable lessons. A man really had to prove himself to Drea and even after that she still had to learn to trust him.

Valarie was still the owner of her salon in Indianapolis but moved on to Atlanta after she got married to a guy named Marcus. She still remembered the death of Sarah like it was yesterday. She knew she had to continue living life, though it did make her feel like she was being selfish. Her and her husband already had two kids and she was pregnant with another one. She stayed in close contact with Eric and Sasha, even made sure she went to see them frequently. Whenever either of them was in Atlanta she had two rooms out of her eight-bedrooms set up specifically for them.

Tim was also sentenced to life in prison, where he stayed in the law library trying to appeal his sentence. Upon arriving to one of Indiana's most notorious prisons Tim had it in his mind that he was about to turn into a savage. He finally got some balls and tried to bully men. It was short lived in Indiana State Prison though as another inmate ran in Tim's room while he was sleep and stabbed him to death. What no one knew about Tim is that he would have rather been dead than sitting in prison the rest of his life anyway. Once Eric heard about Tim getting killed in prison, he was just happy that he suffered before he died. Considering he sat in solitary for four years before being put in population.

Tajuanda was still being the normal Tajuanda. Though she did get married, she still didn't play no games or take any mess from nobody. Her wealth had grown so much that she started feeding hundreds of thousands of dollars into the stock market and letting it grow. She was like another mother to Sasha and Drea. She had them both rooms in her mansion and they were the only ones with the keys to their rooms, not even Tajuanda or her husband had one.

Eric and Kim were like the couple of the century. It seemed that they couldn't go a minute without seeing each other. They had two kids by this time and all five kids were treated the same by Eric. To say that they were wealthy was an understatement. They were very well off. They took vacations whenever they wanted, Eric even got to take his dream trip to Vatican City. Eric opened his battered women shelter called "Ruby's Place." He named it after his grandmother as he always wanted to do. He was also able to open his youth center for troubled teens as he always wanted to do. The youth center was in remembrance of his nephew who died at the early age of seventeen. He named the youth center after his nephew's initials, "DDJ's Helping Hand." He treated Kim so good that she sometimes questioned if she deserved to be treated so good. They were a true power team.

Nathan and Rebecca eventually got married. Rebecca worked from home and ran her own business, while still co-running businesses with Sasha. Her and Sasha were living their dream of writing their first movie. They chose to write about the whole deal with Nick coming into Sasha's life making a bad impact. They were making it motivational though by saying what she did to overcome the whole situation. They had plans of this movie becoming a hot topic, so they were taking their time with writing it. Nathan had taken the enterprise to a new level. Nathan turned into a very smart businessman, he had money to buy his own business, but he was dedicated to where he started from. He stayed planted where he felt his foundation was at and that was with the enterprise. Plus, with Rebecca having so much going on another business seemed far-fetched. They had a daughter and named her Princess, who was their new pride and joy.

Sasha moved her mother in with her, the two of them together along with Jamal just enjoyed life. Sasha was enjoying all her wealth. She bought vacation homes in Arizona, Florida and California. She was now in charge of Tajuanda's Realty company, along with being the co-owner of even more businesses of her own. She spoke to many women all over the United States who were troubled by men. She was truly a diamond who came from the rough. She lost all contact with Nick after his sentencing date but did always wonder if he asked God for forgiveness for all the wrong, he had done to others.

Sasha did have male friends after the whole ordeal with Nick, but she wasn't naïve like she once was. She let them know off top that she didn't want no commitment and if it was meant to be it would just fall into place. Letting them know that she didn't even want to conversate about a relationship. She had been in close contact with Toni, as he made it his duty to find her. He tried to get her to marry him, but Sasha just wouldn't budge. She did love Toni to death, but she just couldn't deal with a man who lived the lifestyle he lived. Toni told her while they were vacationing in Puerto Rico that he would give up the cartel to be with her. She told him she wasn't ready but if it happened, she wouldn't hold back. On two occasions they did make love, but Sasha didn't let the good love making cause her to slip and fall in love.

Nick was laying back in his cell reading a letter that Tonya had written him. He was already upset because he received a family picture of Kim and Eric with his children. Then when he got the letter from

Tonya, he knew he had to do what he had to do to get out of prison and kill everyone on his list. Tonya told him that Sasha and Toni were seeing each other. He cried at first, but then his tears turned into pure anger. He wanted them dead by any cost. The DEA had come to him before telling him that he could get out of prison before his outdate. Nick was never a snitch, but now he was going into the counselor's office to ask if he could call the DEA's office. With other charges hanging over his head he didn't know what the outcome would be, but he was willing to see.

THE END

FROM THE AUTHOR

Though this book is a work of my imagination, I wrote this book to let every woman know that you can bounce back from any situation in life. Not just a bad situation with a man neither. In life, you have a choice, one is to let your past take you out the game and the other choice is to make your past put you in the game. Never let nothing or no one take you out the game, you can bounce back from any situation if your mind is made up to do so. As you can see Sasha was just an innocent lady like most women are, who got caught up with the wrong man. It's on you to learn from your lesson and turn it into your blessing. The key is to learn from that lesson and to never go down the path of that same lesson again.

Contact me for book signings, speaking engagements,

or just some uplifting words at:

ericw8403@gmail.com